T0151053

Romance of Romance

By the Same Author

Hypyhypothesis. Cadmus Editions, San Francisco, 2005

Philosophie Thinly Clothed and Other Stories. Cadmus
Editions, San Francisco, 2003

Romance of Romance

Heather Folsom

Cadmus Editions
San Francisco

Printed in the United States of America
This book is printed on acid-free paper

Cover illustration from Begritten by A. Shapiro, with permission
Cover design by Nina Krebs
Text illustration production by Colleen Dwire

First Edition / Spring 2008

Cadmus Editions
Post Office Box 126
Belvedere Tiburon
California 94920
http://www.cadmuseditions.com
e-mail: jeffcadmus@aol.com

Folsom, Heather Jean
Library of Congress Catalogue Number: 2008927144
ISBN13: 978-0-932274-70-0

10 9 8 7 6 5 4 3 2 1

Contents

Prooemia

First Prologue

SYNS WOKE UP EARLY, MISERABLE and without passion. The writer glanced out the small window of the cottage; the twilight before dawn was a uniform gray.

Lying in bed thinking. Once there had been so much hope, so much determination. Followed by success: hollow, putative.

How had it come to this, that a new ale was the only bright spot of the day, of the entire future. Everything reduced to a quest for deliverance unto oblivion.

But didn't Syns at least have admirable values? Wasn't that, in the end, the most important thing? What were they again? Something about equality . . . something about humanit . . . zzz . . .

Prologue II - Notes on Language

THIS BOOK IS WRITTEN in the argot of H-town. For those unfamiliar with its particular grammatical constructions, a few comments follow.

The "habit of the plural." Even when referring to one person you would say they or them, and we and us for first person. Verbs usually match plural subjects.

You will never see gendered pronouns.

Someone, anyone, everyone, and no one, are plural. Collective nouns are often plural, such as society, crowd, and so forth. Body, heart, and mind are plural.

Several nouns and pronouns are singular or plural depending on context. Examples include soul, life, it, that, and various emotions.

It should be added that different speakers have their own subtle variants of the argot, and that, like any living tongue, vernacular forms abound.

The passage below illustrates some of these principles:

Vus were feeling light-hearted. They sang as they walked. They came upon the clerk Los.

The clerk were frequently glancing over their shoulder. "It're terrible. We have never been so frightened. Our mind are troubled and our body are beginning to break down. Someone are following us but no one believe us and a crowd are laughing behind our back."

Prologue III - A Brief History

SEVERAL DECADES AGO the psychologist Doctor Hans began petitioning the government for assistance in bringing to fruition a cherished dream. Resultant from the doctor's harrying, a grant was eventually bestowed which included funding and three decaying barracks on an abandoned army base. Thus the doctor's wish became reality and CSII, the Center for the Study of the Hermaphrodite, was born.

Hermaphrodites of all ages were invited to be examined. Syns were four years old at the time, in the youngest cohort of the Longitudinal Study. Syns' parents brought them to the Center for the requested week in summer, hoping to justify to themselves their anomalous begetting.

The child subjects and their parents had quarters on the second floor of a stale-smelling building at the edge of a rather sickly forest. Young Syns were on a rollaway bed, their parents had a double in the same drab room. Every day Syns were taken into one of several identical rooms downstairs where various tests were administered, usually involving the arranging of pictures or blocks. There was always a doctor present, wearing a long white coat, deadly serious or falsely jocular, invariably carrying a clipboard.

They returned the next summer. The second year and thereafter they remained two weeks. By the third year Syns knew the other child subjects and gradually they began to feel at home.

In the history of H-town these early years came to be known as the First Period, Under the Radar.

Syns were a precocious child who, by four years of age, could read. By six no book was too advanced. They discovered the center library. Its medical books were used in a game Syns invented: a child would let a book fall open at random, then the children would look at the revealed photograph, horrified and fascinated, and try not to scream. In truth they all wondered about their connection to the naked freaks standing next to measuring sticks in the grainy black and white pictures. Ostensibly the children were happily coloring and reading in the Children's Corner—at its low round table and small chairs painted in primary colors.

Syns found the medical journals and read them thoroughly. They discovered that in Psychology, even in the

Psychology of Abnormal Development, subdivision Sexual Anomalies, there was never more than a paragraph about H's every few months. Findings were always preliminary and tentative: current research could best be regarded as an undertaking that might someday provide an understanding of the character structure and intrapsychic disturbances unique to the hermaphrodite. Most of the articles listed Doctor Hans as first author.

Doctor Quiss, a short thin psychologist, wore thick glasses which magnified unfriendly eyes. When Quiss spoke to the children it was to say "Break the seal and begin now," "Raise a hand if a new pencil is required," and "Put down the pencil and close the book now," in a harsh monotone. The children whispered to each other, "Don't argue with Doctor Q."

For reasons never fully understood, Quiss got in touch with L—— magazine and suggested that the public had a Right to Know about H-town. Journalists from L——, always looking for a good story with compelling pictures, came to CSH the following summer.

A row took place when they arrived. Doctor Hans and some other heretofore quiet and measured psychologists started yelling. After awhile the children were told to come down to the library.

The Children's Corner was flooded with lights. The child subjects were instructed to sit at the table and hold crayons as if they were coloring. This went on for a long time while hundreds of photographs were taken. Quiss hovered around, trying to get into all the shots. When someone tried to ask a child a question, Hans shouted, "Okay, get the hell out now!" The journalists left quickly.

Later the children discussed the incident. Syns wondered privately if it had something to do with Ratting Out, which, in their experience, was the principal reason adults got angry and started yelling.

Six months later the January seventh issue of L— contained a photograph of the children at the table. No names were mentioned. The picture was black and white and, surprisingly, a bit dark. No one at school recognized Syns. The article did not appear to have much of an impact.

But when the family returned to CSH that summer there were several changes. What came to be known as the Second Period, After-L—, had begun.

Formerly, taxis came directly to the barracks and let the families out. Now there was a guard in the booth at the base entrance and a clearance was required before you could enter.

There were many more cars in the parking lot. The two other barracks were opened up. A sign on the building on the left said Housing Quarters, the middle building said Research Center, and the right-hand building said Visitors Center.

Syns and family went into Housing Quarters. It smelled the same as the prior building. Their room was identical to their old room: same metal bed, squeaky rollaway, brown blankets, gray-white sheets, half-flat pillows.

Syns' parents put their suitcases down and went back out into the hall. A parent was saying that because of the grant money, low security clearance, and the public's right to know, there would henceforth be visitors and tours.

Researchers led the tours. They didn't allow photographs and didn't allow visitors to talk to the children. Once in awhile a child would run into a visitor in the bathroom, who would politely ask how it felt to be a hermaphrodite. The child would say, "It're just normal for us." The visitor would smile and nod and some even appeared to have tears in their eyes.

The summer of the visitors Syns vowed that when they grew up they would be a psychologist at CSH. It wasn't perfect but it was the happiest place they knew, where they had friends who—though no one were just like them—were more like them than anywhere else.

The next summer there were further changes.

The Refreshment Stand was situated next to the sidewalk that led to Visitors. It was a slightly dirty white tent with red plastic flags flying from its corners. A flap was lifted in front revealing a white counter. Syns and family went to the stand after dropping off their luggage.

They were the first ones there. The parents murmured that perhaps it was only for bona fide visitors or staff. Syns asked the person behind the counter if they were allowed to get some ice cream.

"Of course. Buy anything you want." They all had cokes and ice cream bars. The parents were having such a good time they sent Syns over to Research on their own. Seated at a big desk was a receptionist. Before, a psychology student in a short version of the long white coat had sat at a small metal table. Syns signed in, said hello to people, and answered the usual questions.

Researchers, subjects, and parents had always taken their meals in the dining room, a bad-smelling place with tan walls, fake-wood-topped tables, brown linoleum, buzzing lights, and awful food in compartments in metal trays. Hardly anyone talked except the researchers. The children would try to keep their spirits up by making noises and laughing behind their napkins.

Syns started down the hall to the dining room but the receptionist called out that the Cafeteria was open over at the Visitors Center.

The cafeteria was painted and bright. It didn't smell terrible. The floor was red linoleum tiles, waxed and shiny. The table-tops were formica, turquoise with tan squiggles. On the wall was a big painting of bears in a meadow in front of a snow-capped mountain. Above the painting was a banner that said Welcome and next to it was the flag in a stand.

Syns' parents were crypto-socialists. Syns suspected that they would find the picture, banner, and flag in bad taste. Syns, however, liked the painting. At the same time socialism was one of the few beliefs of their parents they agreed with, since it was obvious that capitalism was going to benefit only a few people while it hurt many more. But you didn't talk about it outside the family.

There were trays to put plates on and you could choose your food. The servers gave Syns what they asked for.

Syns saw Ues having lunch with their parents and went over and joined them. The food tasted better, everyone were talking. A few psychologists were there but mostly the room was filled with visitors. Syns' parents entered. They saw Syns and waved and smiled. They got their food and joined in. It was the happiest meal of Syns' life.

Visitors were everywhere. They broke loose from the tours and wandered in the woods. Have an ice cream, take a hike, have a meal, take a tour. Doctor Hans and some of the other researchers scowled, but most people seemed more cheerful. For the first time CSII was more like a summer camp and less like a research project you took your abnormal child to.

Everything went on more or less the same for several years.

One day Syns' parents received a letter informing them that permanent residency was being offered to the subjects of the Longitudinal Study in order to facilitate more in-depth investigations. Additionally, for the child subjects, several new educational methods would be implemented and studied.

Syns were twelve, the youngest age accepted. They

begged to go. Their parents had reservations: on one hand they worried about Approaching Adolescent Years as a Freak of Nature, on the other hand they worried about Being Too Sheltered. There were phonecalls to the center. Finally it was decided that the family would go in the summer as usual and then if Syns still wished, they could Stay On.

A humorous moment, to Syns, occurred during a phonecall when one of their parents asked, "Will there be separate dormitories for the gir—oh never mind."

The family arrived for the summer program. Picnic tables were everywhere, next to the stand and back a little ways into the forest. There was a new parking lot next to Visitors just for tour busses.

At the end of two weeks the parents left. Syns and most of the other child subjects remained. The visitors tapered off. The stand was closed. The cafeteria remained open but there were no longer food choices.

School opened in Visitors. The children's bedrooms were upstairs, along with a monitor. The adult permanents stayed in Housing and the researchers who lived on the base stayed upstairs in Research.

Fols were the youngest permanent adult subject, seventeen years old, a child prodigy and graduate student. Their university was allowing them to stay at the center while they worked on their dissertations for triple Ph.D.'s— in Abnormal Psychology, Economics, and Political Science. Fols asked endless questions and never stopped talking about their interests. Syns thought Fols were a bit like themselves in terms of curiosity but the graduate student were much more vocal and hyper.

Fols and Hans liked each other and had things in common: both disliked Quiss, for example. And of course Fols' intelligence and verbosity made them an excellent research subject.

Child subject Brels routinely foiled the monitor and wandered around the base at night. They noticed some light coming from a window upstairs in Housing, very late. The next night the same light was on. They entered the building and crept upstairs. When they heard adult voices they ran back outside. They reported their discovery to the other children. The next night they all sneaked out and followed Brels.

They heard people talking about change and improvement and Fols' excited voice saying "revolution" and "Haven't we given enough? Haven't we provided enough to science? We're called subjects but aren't we actually *objects*? We can be a *force*. We have minds, we have hearts, we have *will*. We can prevail."

Syns were thrilled.

Someone asked, "And do what?"

Fols answered, "First we have to cultivate our ambition. Then we must crystallize a plan. After that it's a simple process of enactment." Dazzling.

"But we'd lose our grant money."

Income was generated from the visitors via donations,

the stand, the cafeteria, and informational booklets. Some of that money, along with small stipends from the government, was given to the adult permanents. The children received no stipends but school and room and board were free.

"Let's think big! Let's get rid of the psychologists and take over!" said Fols.

"Hurrah!"

"Sshh."

Voices became hushed but the children could still hear everything. Everyone were weary of the psychologists but many were afraid of losing their grants and the base.

The discussion went on until the small hours. Finally the children had to return to their quarters for wake-up. But they came back every night to listen.

Then one night child subject Bos sneezed.

Fols opened the door. "Who're out there? Kids! Jees! Go get back in bed, okay?"

The children, devoted to Fols, complied. But they were back the next night. A guard were standing outside Fols' room. "Hey! What are you doing?"

Syns begged, "Please. We want to be part of the revolution."

Fols opened the door. "Again? Okay, hurry up and come in. Jees."

The meetings went on for weeks. The children would fall asleep off and on. It took a long time to reach decisions. There would be near-agreement, then someone would voice an objection and everyone would disagree with that, and then someone else would say, "Perhaps they have a point."

Yet despite the tedium it became, not a matter of whether or not to have a revolution, but a matter of how to accomplish it and how things would be afterwards.

The major arguments were over money and structure—how they could continue if the government pulled its grants and how they were going to live together in some sort of order and harmony.

The leading solution to the money problem was the visitors, who would probably continue to pay to see H's. The basic plan was to get rid of the psychologists, keep the buildings, and increase the visitors. Gys, who were interested in money—as opposed to Fols, who were interested in economics—kept saying, "We need an angle." Many angles were discussed.

Rus, an adult who had been quiet the entire time, said, "What if we stop thinking about what the visitors might want and think about what *we* want."

It was a moment that changed the course of history.

Bos, the sneezer, raised their hand. Up until then the children had not said one word at the meetings.

"Yes?" said Fols.

"Uh."

"You want to say something?"

"Uh. Yeah. Why not do something *fun*."

"Like what?"

"Why not have, uh, an amusement park?"

The adults did not agree to the idea immediately. Someone said there were plenty of amusement parks already. But the idea was included in the discussions from then on. A few meetings later, Phos, another heretofore silent adult, said quietly, "I've always wanted to live in medieval times. Knights and so forth."

In the end almost everyone were in favor of a theme park. Many suggestions were put forward: Commune-town (suggested by Fols), Farm-town, Arts-town, Wild West-town, Dance-town, Prison-town, Medieval-town, Candy-town, Spooky-town, University-town, Future-town, and Beer Garden-town.

It was finally decided that there would be three divisions: Medieval-town, Future-town, and, for those who were opposed to the whole theme park idea, Normal-town.

Committees were formed. On Medieval-town were Syns, Bos, Phos, and some others. It met after dinner at a picnic table in the woods. The nightly meetings in Fols' room became more focused as the committees made their reports.

The next big decision had to do with how profits, if any, would be handled. One night Syns raised their hand.

"What is it?" asked Fols.

"Why don't we just share all the profits equally, no matter what anybody do?"

The comment was met with silence. But after the

silence no one objected. Fols looked like they were trying to contain their enthusiasm so as not to jinx the idea.
"What do you think, Gys?"

"Well, we foresee problems. But we could try it."

There was a vote and everyone said aye.

Next was the question of how to fund the transition.
Gys stood to inherit some money and thought they could
probably persuade their family to release some of it early.
Others started thinking about relatives who might do
the same. Parents of the children seemed particularly
promising.

A financial committee were formed, chaired by Gys.
Two nights later the draft of a letter was passed around,
asking whether—should the government withdraw their
grant or the psychologists have enough data—family
members would be willing to help out their H-loved-one
with a donation to fund the transition to a fully financially
self-sufficient H-town. It was approved after only one night
of discussion.

The letter went out and pledges for donations began
to come in. As predicted, the children's parents were the
most responsive group.

Syns' parents, however, were cautious. They called
Syns and talked about Prudence and the Rainy Day. In
the end they sent back the letter with a checkmark next
to the smallest recommended amount.

Fols wanted to tell the psychologists to leave, Gys
wanted to have a meeting with the government, and

the children wanted a confrontation, especially with Doctor Q. They wanted to shout "Close the booklet and get out now."

Gys' idea was agreed upon. A delegation were formed: Fols, Gys, Bos, and Trys—an adult from a wealthy family that had made a big pledge.

It was noon in mid-October. Almost everyone were in the cafeteria. The menu was fish sticks with tartar sauce, canned spinach, a sprig of pale purple grapes with seeds, milk in a carton, a cupcake with white frosting, and a cube of red jello.

A teachers asked, "Where're Bos?"

Often a child might be in the bathroom or just having a moment to themselves. But for some reason a humming began among the teachers, "Where're Bos?" "Where're Bos?"

Quiss came over where the children were sitting and said, "Speak up. What has been done to child subject Bos?"

Someone fired the first shot. A cupcake hit Quiss in the glasses. All the children, their frustration finally unleashed, joined in with fish sticks, tartar sauce, spinach, milk, grapes, more cupcakes, and jello. The teachers were shouting so the children pelted them too. Some of the adult permanents began throwing food, possibly some of the researchers. Everyone got covered so it was difficult to tell who the abstainers were.

The delegation had just gotten into a taxi in front of

Housing. Syns ran over, pounded on a window, and yelled that a foodfight was underway. At least Fols and Bos rushed in and joined the fray.

Under the bear painting was a microphone on a stand. Fols turned it on. "We had planned to do this differently but circumstances have altered things. All psychologists are to leave the premises immediately. CSH is closed. H-town, run by all of *us*, is now open."

Three police officers skidded in. They arrested Fols who—shouting "revolution"—went limp and had to be dragged across the swampy floor. An officer asked who started the fight and the children pointed to Q, indeed the most saturated, reeling behind food-coated glasses. They led Quiss away too.

An officer said, "Everyone sit down and stay where you are. We'll be taking statements. The teachers may take the children out."

The children took showers and put on dry clothes. Grilled cheese sandwiches and apples were sent over.

The weekend was quiet. Mostly everyone slept. Syns' parents called. They had heard about the foodfight on the news and were coming to get them. Syns persuaded them to wait.

Around eleven a.m. on Monday a limousine pulled up in front of Research. Several official-looking strangers got out and went inside.

Shortly after one p.m. the strangers came into the classroom. The children had been discussing how to behave. They were concerned that if they looked too upset the government might shut everything down, but if they seemed too happy it might look like they had No Remorse. They had decided to look moderately cheerful. When asked, they said they loved it at CSH. Nothing like the cafeteria fight had ever happened before. They knew nothing about how it started. The officials asked where Bos had been and everyone said they thought Bos were probably in the bathroom. Bos concurred.

Later a police car arrived and Fols and Quiss got out. They went into Research. Hours passed. School was over for the day but everyone stayed in the classroom, anxiously waiting to find out what would happen next.

Suddenly a voice boomed from the loudspeaker, "Everyone report to the dining room in the Research Center for an important announcement."

They filed into the dim dining room where there was no food anymore, just the old bad smell, slightly fainter. The room had a small stage on which the officials were standing.

Syns were trying to listen but they were so nervous they only caught phrases: ". . . came to a head . . . discussion going on for some time . . . enough data exist . . . live subjects no longer needed . . . transformation to unsupported . . . special needs . . . hermaphrodite community . . . not wish to obstruct . . . encourage initiative . . . proposal to allow land use and development . . . no special tax considerations . . . must have economically viable . . .

institute dissolved . . . grants terminated . . . apply for university or private grants to analyze . . . children appear healthy . . . no criminal investigation . . ."

No one spoke. The officials left. The researchers filed out. Everyone else sat still, wondering what was about to take place.

Fols jumped onto the stage. "We don't need to go. We have the pledge money. We can keep the utilities going and the staff in place while work begins."

People nodded but no one cheered because it was a very bad day for the researchers.

Fols looked over at the children. "What do you all want?"

"Stay," "Oh gods stay," "Please please stay," et cetera.

Fols said, "We'll try."

Giving impetus to the children's staying was the fact that the revolution depended heavily on their parents' pledge money.

Gys were in charge of contacting the parents. They brought the children into the office one by one. Researchers were packing up, saying nothing.

Syns' were last, probably due to the size of their parents' pledge. Gys spoke into the phone: ". . . school will remain open . . . continuity of education . . . same teachers, same monitor . . . same quarters . . . as little disruption as possible . . . learning . . . hands-on experience . . . welcome part of the new structure . . . visitor education program . . . hope of the future . . ."

Syns got on the phone and said they wanted to stay more than anything. They reiterated that of course they didn't participate in the foodfight and added, "You know how the capitalist media gets everything wrong."

Syns' parents were saying it was best to wait until things were More Settled but eventually they capitulated. The foodfight was briefly in the news and protractedly in the TV comedy routines. Bos were invited to speak on the radio. They talked about Medieval-town and how children everywhere should get their parents to bring them so they could see that H's weren't any different from anyone else. Bos were charming and brought in more donations. Thus the Third Period, Revolution, came to an end.

The Fourth and final Period, Towns, was an era of construction—of the theme park and of a way of life. There were a host of problems.

First was anti-climax. Everyone were eager to get started with building but fall would soon be advancing to winter. H's scraped by, trying not to use up the donations, doing a lot of planning. Medieval-town would be opened first. Profits from it would be used to build Future-town and Normal-town.

The architect Kriks arrived, a successful outsider who turned out to be an H.

A skirmish took place over authenticity. Purists wanted to choose a date and place in the Middle Ages and recreate it as closely as possible. Kriks were opposed. They thought that since this was to be a theme park, the best features should be culled from all periods and places. Meetings were held. Kriks eventually prevailed. As a compromise an Educational Museum was added.

Related to authenticity were issues of sanitation, electricity, and other aspects of modern convenience. The greatest battle raged over the matter of armor: some wanted it made from aluminum. Though far less protective than steel, it was much lighter and easier to maintain. At one point debate ran so high there was discussion of a split into Old Medieval-town and New Medieval-town. It never happened, but the name Old M came into common use. The purists won the battle of armor; the progressives, of plumbing.

The spring thaw came at last. In response to their pleas, the children were allowed to start school at seven a.m. so that they could be done by two and help out.

A castle went up with a curtain wall, drawbridge, moat, portcullis, bailey, stables, kitchens, tower, and a large rectangular hall with oilleted cross-shaped arrow loops, crenellated parapets, and machiolated bastions and bartizans projected over the walls on chamfered corbels. It began with a frame of steel and wood. This was followed by wooden walls, then a formed cement exterior and plaster interior, shaped and painted to look like old stones and ashlars. Nearby were the pastures, stables, tournament field, and village—with its alehouse, smithy, shops, and thatched cottages.

Old M was opened to the public in midsummer. H's could be seen in period dress at work on a forge, making pies and pasties, spinning, weaving, dyeing, and engaging in crafts and enterprises that were enjoyable to do and observe and, whenever possible, provided things for sale. There were a parade of knights and a joust. From the start it was a great success.

Future-town was planned to abut Old M on the right, Normal-town on the left. Kriks, now a permanent, were again the architect. As summer turned into the second post-revolutionary fall, sounds of construction rang out in the crisp medieval air.

Normal and F-town opened the following summer. N included tract houses, a park with a duck-pond, a two-hole golf course, and a downtown with several buildings, including City Hall. Surprising to some, N was highly popular with the visitors; they were fascinated to observe H's going about the conventional activities of daily life. F included rides, various restaurants, and a hermaphrodite zoo.

There was a much-discussed court case at the time regarding whether H-town was educational and whole-some enough for visits from public school children on state sponsored field trips. The case was expedited to the highest court in the land. Lawyers for H-town presented testimony from founding parents stating their belief that H-town represented a model community in opposition to discrimination. Further, their children were no worse than anyone else's and had a right to learn to make a living and so forth. The Educational Museum was highlighted, as was the fact that a functioning elementary and high school existed in the Visitors Center. Finally, the questionable educational value of extant field trips to more standard amusement parks was highlighted. The vote was close but the pro arguments prevailed. Thereafter, the busloads of school children were a staple of H-town economy, especially during winter months when the tourist season was over and school discounts abounded.

Residents could live in any of the three towns. Most chose to live in Normal, including many who worked in F. M-town residents overwhelmingly chose to live in the cottages and castle of Old M.

Mythic Sex

Television comedians did much to keep H-town in the public eye and inadvertently enhanced its success. Many people attributed to the comedians the burgeoning interest in H-sex, or what came to be called Mythic Sex.

The Myth was that because of II's various anatomies they were capable of greatly superior sex and assortments of pleasure. For awhile it looked like the school tours were going to be stopped. This was serious enough to spur a round of meetings.

There were four camps of opinion:

The Education Camp. They disliked the Myth and

wanted to devote energy to educating the world about what H-sex were really like.

The Conservative Economic Camp. On the surface they appeared to be in agreement with the Educationalists but in fact they were indifferent to the Myth and only wanted it minimized in order to preserve the school tours and the revenue generated by conservative visitors.

The Extreme Economists. They wanted to exploit the Myth for profit and had a potpourri of ideas as to how this might be done—everything from pornographic films and no-holds-barred magazines and books, to entertainments which were basically variants of prostitution, in which the paying visitor either watched something transpire or participated.

The Ego Camp. They loved the Myth and wanted it promoted because it was so flattering.

An early proposal was to divide permanently into these camps as had been done with the three towns, but it was soon abandoned.

What happened was a compromise of sorts. Exploitation of the Myth was initiated on a limited basis. The truth was, almost no one wanted to turn the place into Orgy-town. The H-children were a big draw, not to mention the donations they continued to inspire. It was hoped that by limiting the commercial application of the Myth, the field trips could continue and the children of H-town would be allowed to stay. The final plan was to limit the promotion of the Myth to the publication of H-romance novels which were to be at least semi-tasteful.

The Extreme Economists who wanted more flamboyant forms of exploitation were disgruntled, the Educationalists who wanted to repudiate the Myth were disappointed, the Conservative Economists were guardedly pleased, the Egoists were delighted.

The plan was more brilliant than anyone could have imagined: the market for H-romances proved limitless. It was only a few years before income from the books outdistanced all other sources, including revenues from the tournaments.

The number of writers kept increasing in order to feed the outside world's insatiable craving for Mythic H-romance. And not just the outside world—a substantial throng of hungry readers lived within the H-town gates.

Syns graduated from H-town High School. They were old enough to move out of Visitors. They chose Old M where they had been assisting at the smithy since its creation, and began hammering fulltime. They obtained a B.A. in Liberal Arts and an M.A. in History via correspondence courses.

At one time they had wanted to become a psychologist, then a revolutionary. When the revolution succeeded they were unclear about their goals. Eventually they were talked into writing an H-romance, as were many young people coming into the employment market. Syns' first book, *The Double Jewels in the Double Crowns*, was an instant bestseller, which has remained on the list of top-selling H-romances ever since. Thus Syns found, entirely by accident, their life's work.

Their exclusively medieval novels enhanced Old M's prestige. Though retiring by nature they were more than moderately famous.

Interviewers from the outside often asked Syns how they felt about making the same income as everyone else in H-town. In truth it was one of the few things they felt good about. Successful writers who felt differently moved out; some became immensely wealthy. But in income generated, Syns outdistanced all other H-romance writers, both inside and out.

Divisions

Life in H-town settled into routine. Additions were made, such as the ice rink and shopping mall in N, the midway and space diner in F, and the cathedral and knight school in M.

Then trouble erupted in Normal. Under its placid surface was a restless faultline: most residents wanted the town to stay set in the time period in which it was built, a time which became more outdated with each passing year. A minority wanted to keep it up-to-date.

The tectonic plates finally heaved asunder, resulting in a split into Old Normal and New Normal. Old Normal remained exactly as it was. Land between it and the back of Housing and further to the left became New

Normal. It had mini-skyscrapers, a mini-freeway, and the latest technologies. Several businesses moved there, notably H-town Publishing.

Most people chose to stay in Old N. On weekends, when businesses tended to be closed, New N was practically a ghost town. It was the least popular section with the visitors.

For all the compromises that were successfully made at H-town—after all, if there was one thing H's were good at, it was seeing multiple sides of an issue—there existed a division that remained unbridgeable. The outside world assumed that a given H tended to identify with one gender more than another. The assumption was false. But there were, in fact, two groups. The differentiating factor was this: height. The taller you were, the more desirable, the shorter, the less.

The matrix of pairings involving talls and shorts was as follows:

Tall with tall. The ideal.

Short with short. The most common, due to the fact that there were many more shorts than talls.

Tall with short. Rare, but it happened from time to time, almost always because the short had some compensating quality, such as intelligence, a good nature, a great sense of humor, and so forth. But the tallest never took up with a short under any circumstances.

Until Syns were fourteen it looked like they were going to be a tall. Their parents were short but Syns were shooting upwards. No one gave it much thought, including Syns. Suddenly they stopped growing. Their fate were sealed along with their epiphyses. They didn't mind. They felt the tall-short issue was mildly ridiculous. "What difference do it make?" they would ask. "Do one really need to see over more hedges?"

But Syns did have an inferiority complex. It was there when they had assumed they were going to be a tall. It was there when they became a short. It had nothing to do with being an H. It was this: they felt they were unattractive and always would be. It was their painful secret.

Later, after many partners, they realized that some people did seem to find them desirable, and granted it was possible that they were at least slightly attractive. But it was always shaky.

When our story begins, Syns weren't involved with anyone, it didn't seem crucial. After a few drinks they were apt to say, "We've had enough great sex for one lifetime."

Prologue IV - Resumption

LET US RETURN THEN, to Syns, lying in bed on August first, day of the High Summer Tournament, miserable and without passion. Time passed while we presented the background—dawn had arrived and then collapsed under the weight of gray, allowing a light drizzle to seep through like perspiration. The cathedral bells rang out ten a.m. They were late.

They got up and put on their costume. Every citizen of M-town had a part to play at the tournaments. Syns' job as a serf was to mingle in the crowd, sit in the cheapest seats at the joust, and act in a loutish manner. The role suited them well but they had wearied of it years before. Were it not for the new ale, they would, as usual, have skipped the event entirely.

They headed out from their cottage on a narrow path. It was deserted but the oppressive sounds of festival day crowded the air: jabbering tourists, strident hawkers, trumpet blast and peacock shriek.

The path joined the high street—winding and cobbled, with shops leaning out over it—which led up to the tournament field and the castle beyond. It was brutally packed. Syns crammed into the mob. A tourist trod on their foot and said nothing.

Eventually the banners of the ale tent came into view, flopping disconsolately in the wet breeze like dying fish. The ale tent was one of the largest, positioned near the entry to the field. A long line had formed, Syns joined its rear.

Livs and Lucs jumped toward them, personal pewter tankards in hand, in their duo-jester outfit. The duo-jester were meant to be a satiric depiction of the H. One grotesque and garish outfit covered two persons, allowing two heads to pop out of the top and an arm and leg apiece. The last was accomplished by having each participant's legs held together in a padded stocking. To move about they had to take turns jumping. The two heads squabbled over everything. In real life Livs and Lucs were shy librarians at Research.

"What took you so long?" Livs called out.

"By the way, we don't care," interjected Lucs.

"Nothing," said Syns.

"'Tis well worth the effort, a highly drinkable brew," Livs said loudly.

"Zounds and curses, we have to agree with you on this one point. But no other," Lucs declaimed.

Already a significant number of people were in line behind Syns. The duo-jester cut in as usual. "Don't cut ye in line!" chided Livs. Then to the onlookers, "Pardon us, entirely their fault, but what can we do?"

The line inched forward while the drizzle ceased and shadows began crawling over the damp ground. The duo ingratiated themselves with the crowd while Syns stared ahead. Waiting in line were filled with anxiety. The closer you got the more likely your chances of getting a pint before they ran out. But the likelihood also increased that the barrels would sputter just when it was your turn.

At last they were in the diffused light of the white canvas tent. The dirt floor was littered with plastic cups, gray and embossed to resemble tankards. The smell of brew was sickeningly strong.

An archer were directly in front of them. The barrel dribbled out a few drops and died.

"Jimes, Anches, anything left in your barrels?"

No and nay.

"Sorry. Worse luck."

The poor archer quivered, loosed a volley of curses, and crept away.

"That's it, then," sighed Livs.

"You each got pints already," muttered Syns.

"Two apiece actually," said Lucs with a smile.

"No wonder they ran out."

"What do ye want to do? Shall we go watch the joust?" asked Livs.

Anything but the joust, thought Syns. There was nothing like repeatedly writing about something, to remove any shred of appeal.

Behind them the line dissipated into nothingness as the sad word was passed along. Livs and Lucs were jumping toward the opening of the tent. Syns stood rooted in despair.

"Hells, how did this one get by us?" Jimes were rolling a barrel forward. They looked up at Syns. "This must be your lucky day."

They poured a frothing cup and handed it to Syns. The writer-serf took a desperate sip. Ahhh. Heavy, cold, and strong.

The duo whip-turned and bounded over, extending their tankards. The tappers were imbibing as they packed up.

When Syns and the duo finished their pints, Jimes called out, "Another?"

The three sat on a hay bale inside the tent for the next round. For the next they sprawled on the ground, their heads against the bale like wanton harvesters. Someone came over to pour the fourth, saying the barrel was drained and it was time to take down the tent.

Syns looked over at Livs, whose eyes were nearly closed. Lucs' were slightly more open. With mutual assistance they all managed to stand. Leaning on each other they jumped and staggered into the painful brightness outside.

Livs dropped their tankard and slithered to the ground, where they remained. Lucs, pulled along, fell too.

Syns looked around. It was the oddest intoxication they had ever experienced: every object was rimmed in purple.

"We love ale. We really love it. Do ye?" Lucs called up.

"We love it, yes," said Syns.

"We love it more than anything. More than love. Do ye?"

"Love it more than love?" Syns considered. It was easy

for Lucs to say. They had never even experienced the emotion. But as for themselves, did they love this ale more than the love of lovers? "Yes we do. We have had enough love, enough sex, good sex, and great sex, for one lifetime." Or had we? Perhaps we had been a failure at all of it.

"And ye the great expert on romance." The comment was followed by a sputtering snore as Lucs joined their conjoined twin in sleep.

Syns grimaced. The love in our novels are utterly false. Based on ever-more-distant and dimming memories.

They looked up.

And that was the moment. That was the pivot, a matter of pure coincidence, or fate, or folly, upon which life changed.

Final Prologue

IN THEIR LINE OF VISION was the awning-covered section of the grandstand, reserved for the nobility. On the field in front of it were two figures. One had their back to Syns but the black armor and immense size could only be Cyras the Giant Knight. Facing toward Syns were the Sovereign Rels, who threw something at Cyras.

And then Rels turned.

Swiftly, yet in purple-rimmed clarity, the royal robe flared out, the hair whirled below the golden crown. Everything rotated, glinting like diamonds.

Something penetrated Syns' body—dagger, sword, pike. No, it was more like blunt trauma—mace, cudgel, flail. But of greater magnitude—waterfall, avalanche, exploding building's broken walls, circling and plunging.

Words rang out somewhere: "You shall bow down to us. We are your idol, your golden calf. You shall fall to your knees, press your head upon the ground, and worship us."

Syns felt a wave of heat descending, as if someone were pouring melted wax on their head. Their knees buckled. They felt the warm buffer of the duo-jester as the ground came up to receive them and they knew no more.

Book One: Butts Various

Futuretown

LIKE SNOWFLAKES, NO TWO HANGOVERS are alike. But in the bell-shaped curve of hangovers this one was more than a couple of standard deviations out, with qualities Syns had never experienced before.

The headache was mammoth though not woolly. Accompanying it was a sense of lightness, as if their body hovered like a jellyfish trapped in the sunken ship of their head. If the head had been missing they could have floated away on the lightest of currents, flown through the air, jumped twenty feet in the weak grasp of the moon. There was a feeling of gusto, of preposterous optimism.

Livs and Lucs snored beneath them. The field was empty except for food wrappers, cups, programs, souvenirs, and abandoned pieces of clothing. Shadows reclined across the field, bells chimed evensong.

Something growled in their chest like hunger pangs in the wrong area. The world had never looked more beautiful. Even with needles of pain pricking their eyes, they felt a desire to go out into the glorious evening, the great newborn world.

Whither? Home was a gnashing of teeth, a prison—worse, a place of no air.

Futuretown. Have a meal. A few drinks.

Residents were supposed to change into F-town attire before entering but it was a tournament day and no one bothered very much.

Abandoning Livs and Lucs, and not for the first time, they started off toward the M-town–F-town Bridge. A few tourists were still around, calling out the names of lost children. In the air was the smell of diesel and the low lament of buses.

In F they passed a small parking lot surrounded by leafy trees; the dusty, plantless ride area with the roller-coaster and merry-go-round; the midway's unwinnable games; the hermaphrodite zoo where the hippo Augustuss snorted contentedly in their muddy pool; the space diner on its rotating column.

Suddenly they had to sit down. They collapsed onto the nearest bench, put their head in their hands, and wept uncomprehendingly.

They got up and went over to their favorite restaurant, the JetFish Grotto. On entering they were met by the smell of fish and stale cooking oil interlarded with frying burgers and grilling steaks; by dimness of light; by dark wood adorned with dusty fishing nets, glass floats, and model jets. Everything so familiar and comforting they almost wept again.

The restaurant was full but Syns' favorite booth, by the swinging door to the kitchen, was free. Dodging the door they sank down in relief. Soon they were eating fish and fries and drinking scotch and soda and the world was softening back to normality.

H-town had its own television station, WHRM, rejected in Old M but widely viewed in F and the Normals. The

JetFish had a TV half-way down the bar.

"Turn up the sound, turn up the sound!" Syns were standing and shouting.

On the screen the Sovereign looked irritated. Syns raced to the bar. "*Please* turn up the sound!"

A few snickers among the diners.

". . . don't know for how long. We will continue to carry out our duties from there." The picture switched to the anchor. "And that's the surprising news from Old M, where the Sovereign Rels, for reasons they would not disclose, declared at today's High Summer Tournament that they would be retreating into the tower for an indefinite period of time."

The news shifted to joust results and Syns turned away. The tower. It felt like good news somehow. They became aware of their behavior and slunk back to their fish and scotch.

Self-doubt had returned but it contained more peril than usual, a tension almost like excitement—a jig upon the oboe of the mind. Could it possibly be hope? They paid and left.

The summer evening continued to darken. Syns looked up at the tower, the highest point in H-town. Were the Sovereign there? Why? What did it matter?

The right side of their chest was scooped out like the shore after a rough tide; the left side was bursting with all the sand pushed over from the right. A thought: If ever you were to be angry with us, we would be happy, we would be laughing.

They were on the M-F bridge. It was impossible to return to their cottage. Something had shifted. A rockslide had taken place in their soul and the old road home was no longer open.

The Boars' Butts

THE BOARS' BUTTS IN OLD M had been Syns' place of respite—i.e. drinking—for a long time. In fact they had chosen their cottage primarily because of the path that led from their front door to the back door of the alehouse. Thither they now repaired. They were hailed by regulars and the barkeep Stils.

The room was large, low-ceilinged, and dark, with a perpetual smell of ale and smoke. The tables and barstools were packed but there was always room for more.

Syns pushed their way to the bar, ordered a draught of Old Usual and sank their elbows onto the polished wood.

"Made it through another High," remarked Stils. "One more to go. Quite the news about the Sovereign."

A stab in the crowded left chest area. "Yeh."

"Wonder what happened," said Stils.

Wims, a plumber dressed as an acrobat, pressing against Syns' right side, piped up, "Lovers' quarrel, they're saying. There's betting going on about how long they'll keep it up. Care to make a wager?"

"Nah. But why, over what?" Syns tried to sound bored.

"Nobody're talking. Most folks think it were the giant's fault.

Nearby, Fars, a weaver, said, "Couldn't have been Rels. What the hells do they see in that ogre anyway? What do you think, Syns? You're the big expert."

43

"What, us?" Syns forced a laugh. "We're nothing but a hack writer and we know it." This was their stock reply whenever the subject of their profession came up. It never failed to get a laugh. But in truth Syns felt even more fraudulent than usual. Irritated too. For gods' sakes, we're a romance writer for money, not an oracle. Couldn't, for once, we simply be understood? But how could that be, given that we understand ourselves not at all.

"Come on Syns, you must have a theory," urged Fars.

Syns fervently didn't want to discuss it. But suddenly they wanted to hear people talk about love in their own lives. "It're probably not much different than what happen to everybody. Who here haven't had love troubles?"

"Hey!" Fars shouted to the room at large. "Syns are bottom-fishing for material for their next book. Anybody want to bite?"

It was convenient cover and Syns let it ride. "Yeah. Who want to tell us the truth about what happened to them in love?"

"Okay, we'll go first," a guild-clad baker, Pors, offered from across the room. "We may be peculiar," general agreement and laughter, "but we finally figured something out about ourselves. We fall in love over and over. It're easy. But it never last. They always leave us. For a long time we thought there was something wrong with us. Well, in a way that's true," more laughter, "but it wasn't what we thought. The reason they leave is because somehow we brilliantly gauge just who *will* leave us, and that are who we fall for. We call it the Brilliant Gauge."

"But why?" asked Kyrs, a farrier, now at Syns' right because everyone along the bar had turned to face the room.

"We guess you could say we know ourselves too well," answered Pors. "This way we get to fall in love, have the excitement, a bit of pleasure, but not too much, because deep down we know we don't deserve it. The ending is built in, the dues are pre-paid."

Kyrs spoke next. "We do a version of that too. We could look a lot better than we do," laughter, "but we cultivate looking rather bad so people won't fall in love with us. Because whenever they do, we always wind up rejecting them. And we hate doing it."

Trops, a wheelwright standing by the dormant fireplace, said, "We did the opposite. We devoted our life to making ourselves desirable. Plastic surgery, dyeing our hair, making our body flawless. We've had plenty of romance. But something were always amiss. We don't know what it were. Lately we've been wondering if it were the falseness of our appearance. We've started letting our hair grow out and we're thinking of getting a reverse nose job."

A stranger in a voluminous hooded black cape next to Trops spoke next. "In a way, we do the opposite of *you*. Our love affair have always been with ourselves. Yes, we're an H, but we're not sure it're a factor. One thing about this type of relationship is that we can create exactly the lover we want. We have discovered that we are more attracted to ourselves if we look bad, not good. We don't know why. Perhaps we feel more like beasts of the field. At any rate, we are happy with our choice."

Rofs, director of the dance troupe, standing at the back near Pors, said, "Sometimes we ask ourselves 'What have you accomplished in this life?' The answer is 'We never assaulted anyone. We contained our impulses.' That's our greatest achievement."

A stranger in one of the loose robes for sale at the entrance gate sat at a trestle table. "We loved sex so much we got a job as a field researcher. We've devoted our life to studying it. For a long time it were fascinating. But eventually it became a chore."

"We fell in love and we've been together a long time. It're great. Just a little bit boring most of the time." Flys, a chandler, from the end of the bar.

"We pretended to love someone once, so we could get their money. We got it, too. We've never been in love. Can't imagine it." A stranger in courtier's robes at a trestle table.

"Doctor Bans, Ph.D. in Psychology, tenured professor for many years," said a stranger in an executioner's mask. "Our field of expertise is romantic love. We've published extensively. Basically, there are those who admit to falling in love and those who don't. But the data show that it happen to everyone. The ones who don't admit it are worse off. They feel too ashamed. To feel entitled to romantic love require a degree of self-esteem.

Our latest monograph, A Study of Twins—"

"We're just a struggling literary novelist, not a rain-maker like you, Syns." Gans, author and cheesemaker, were standing in the doorway. "All contemporary cultures are organized around sex—it're the top sport, the top consumer enterprise. Sex's biology are feted toward these ends. Attraction are made into something transcendentally meaningful. When we're in love it seem more significant than anything else. But at some point it cool down and we're forced to admit 'This are just one thing among many things.' The admission undermines society. So there's a myth to protect it, the myth of disillusionment. When we begin to see the weak spots in our sex and love lives, same things really, we blame ourselves. We say, 'We did not choose wisely. It were not the right person.' We fall out of love, guiltily, and we fall in love with someone else, guiltily, to restore sex's power. Thus the affair. As you may or may not know, all our novels are about affairs. It's a higher form of literature than your romances, Syns, though much less lucrative. Our sex drive have dominated our lives. And though we write book after book, still we know nothing."

Syns had always thought Gans were a pompous fool. But perhaps they had a bit of awareness after all. At least they admitted their ignorance. We can't stand our books. We also despise our sniveling cynicism. Were we to speak truthfully it would be nothing but apology.

Gans came over and squeezed in at the bar.

The discussion continued, tales of the recovered and non-recovered, the begun and non-begun, the ended and non-ended, along the axes of requition.

"It expired like a poisoned rat."

"It were so strong it burned itself out."

"They changed."

"We changed."

Someone Syns didn't know had been pacing the whole time, threading their way through the crowd, looking more and more agitated. They wore a white robe and had cat-like eyes and a parched, ravenous look.

Syns asked them, "Do you have anything you want to say?"

Gans interposed, "They are Jults. They were in love and were jilted. They never got over it. They went mad."

Others nodded. Jults paced faster.

Coldness flooded Syns' chest. Revealed to themselves was their deepest, most private fear: madness from love gone bad. If you really gave your heart, your whole heart, and things went awry, you would never recover.

A sensation of falling into chaos, an edge crossed. How susceptible we are, have always been.

Somehow, being a romance writer made the discovery all the more humiliating.

Dirt and Sad Parade

MUTTERING THAT THEY HAD TO GO, Syns went behind the bar. They grabbed a bottle of scotch. And having yelled "Tab!" they went out.

Half-way home they stumbled and fell, landing face-down in dirt and leaves. After the shock of impact it was pleasant. There was nowhere further to fall. The ground smelled good, nutlike. It was cool and a bit damp. Chimes tolled the midnight office. An owl hooted.

After awhile Syns bethought themselves to proceed further toward home. Staying low to the friendly ground, they moved by peristalsis. Earthworms had the right idea.

It was all so foreign, as if we had turned into another person. Yet also familiar, as if a version of ourselves from a bygone era had returned. They stopped and clutched at the bosom of earth, face buried even deeper in earth and leaves.

An insect crawled on their cheek. Who care, if we do not care. The dirt docs not care. The bells do not care. And Rels, most definitely, do not care. How embarrassing, to have to be the one to care. About our very survival. For should we cease to care, in an instant we are no more.

They thought for awhile about dying by never getting up again. Inanition. Become an apparition. No need for ammunition.

Longing make you weep. Weeping is, in fact, the one

49

thing you are capable of doing. Unable to go forward or backward, you lie still in misery, paralytic without repose.

A scent of flowers wafted by, strong and comforting as spray-on starch.

Were we ever in love before? Yes. What do that imply for the present time? Let us consider. First love at eight years old. Successful, innocent, loved in return. If only we had stopped then. Second love, ten years old. Hope and hopelessness. The same ever after. The last infatuation—when were it? Can't remember at the moment. The important thing is that it seemed we would perish without them. We didn't. And after awhile we no longer desired them at all. Now it would appear to be Rels. We do not know them. Best to go to home to bed. Wait for this latest error to pass over like a witless shade.

Syns pressed their face still deeper into the dirt, almost suffocating. They began to mutter aloud, "We feel ashamed for even having desire. For needing anything. Not wanting to inflict ourselves on others. Especially if you are unlovable but insist on surviving. And yet this misery are better, somehow, than the way we have been feeling of late. More hellish but more interesting. The re-emergent libido, like wild dogs that get into everything. The pull to regression, anxiety, disorganization, a kind of awakening. White noise of ourselves."

Syns were getting bits of dirt in their mouth. "When love come we must hold on like riders from the steppes, no saddles, grasping onto the horses' rough manes, pressing our legs into their flanks. Or, a dangerous sea creature, some ancient truth, ancient lie, up from the depths to terrify and excite us. Perhaps it will submerge soon and go back out to sea. But when it surface it cannot be ignored. Or, perhaps we are the sea creature. All we know is that we must live for ages in darkness."

Fortunately no one heard these ravings. Eventually they rolled over and faced the sky and spit out dirt for awhile. The big-faced moon behind a tremulous fan of branches and leaves had nothing useful to say.

This was probably the most drinking we have ever done in a single day. Yet sobriety is returning. Feeling like a rejected lover *already*.

"Rels, somewhere in the tower, brushing their teeth, or sleeping, going to the bathroom, having thoughts, dreams. Wholly other. Distant as a figure from history, gone for centuries."

They heard a commotion, a stirring along the path, and sat up. Three ghostlike forms materialized.

"Who go there?" Syns called out.

In response, a horrifying wail.

"Have to give them a shot after all."

"Yeah, no choice."

"Sit them down in case they get woozy."

A moan and then silence.

Someone lit a cigarette. In the matchflare Syns saw Jults. The other two figures were also wearing white. One noticed Syns. "Taking them over to the hospital."

Syns were all the way sober, painfully so, their heart were racing. If this was an omen it was a bad one. The bottle was nearby. They unscrewed the cap and took a burning gulp. "Want some?"

"Love to but can't. On duty."

They made small talk awhile, then the sad parade moved on.

Syns drank until armored within. "Drinking to fall forward. We feel like the Egyptians. Ethanol and the holy fools. Heroic warriors drank from dawn to dusk, or dusk to dawn. Rels, where are *yoooo*?"

They lay back down. Fell asleep for a moment. Awoke with a shiver, nose running, tears falling. They turned around and made their way back to the alehouse.

The Barkeep

SYNS ENTERED THE ALEHOUSE through the back door. The establishment was closed but Stils were there, wiping down the bar.

"Could we talk to you?" Leaves and dirt were cascading to the floor.

"Have a seat."

"You have to swear not to laugh." They sat.

"Barkeep's honor. Shot?"

"Yes please. You promise you won't laugh?"

"Shoot."

"Something happened to us. We've been in a bad mood for a long time. Today we snapped."

"What happened?"

"No laughing now." Syns looked closely at Stils' face. "We saw something—someone—at the tournament. Someone we do not know and will never know. And now we are miserable no matter how much we drink."

"Ah."

"What 'ah'?"

"You have fallen in love."

Despite the fact that Syns had been telling themselves this very thing, hearing it from the barkeep felt like getting a rubbing alcohol massage when you were already cold. "We've been in love before. This are worse."

"Are you sure you've been in love before?"

"Everyone have. You heard the conversation tonight.

Anyway, why now? We know it cannot be. We have no illusions." But the turn the turn the turn. And if this were not falling in love for the first time, it were nonetheless of some more intense and dangerous order than ever before. "Are this our punishment for the shallowness and falseness of our books?"

"It're a normal thing."

Famed Romance Writer Kills Selves Over Broken Heart. Almost tears. We do not shed tears no matter how much we drink. "Or are it something subconscious so we will have something to write about? Do we hate our life because we have nothing to write about anymore?"

"It happened because you are human."

"Because we're an H?"

"A human being. It cannot be escaped."

"What do we *do*? We cannot tell you who they are but we assure you there are no hope. And loving from afar are unendurably painful. And stupid."

"There are always hope if you live on the same planet at the same time in history."

The barkeep's words were a balm. Syns were talking, having a conversation in the real world about . . . it. Had they ever talked of such things before? "But the odds are so low."

"If you don't buy a ticket they are worse."

Everyone bet against us. Why wouldn't they? We are on a tiny path of things that might possibly go right, among the wide boulevards of things that will surely go wrong.

"We're beginning to see why we became a cynic."

"Cynics and comics are romantics underneath. If you never get rejected you're not taking enough chances."

"But what if we don't survive?" An image of Jults. "And what if . . . they . . . get together with someone else?"

"Try anyway. You never know what will happen when you take action."

In the ring, gloved, the body too bruised to go on. Yet you must. Eyes swollen shut. Cut 'em! you call out. The ring of powerlessness, fighting anyway.

Stils added, "They don't know you yet."

Syns felt like a frond of seaweed that had been cast ashore and dried to crispness on the beach. A wave had just covered them. Hydration. Salvation. Better to try and fail . . . hadn't that always been our motto? In everything except love.

"Don't worry about appearing foolish, it can't be helped. If you take action you can be happy, no matter what happens. If you don't take action you cannot be happy, no matter what happens." Stils were expostulating and pouring shots, counselor and pharmacist.

"You have transformed my situation from nightmarish imaginings to a terrible fact in the world."

The barkeep smiled. "Progress. Time to close up."

Syns feared the vampirine deadness lurking in their cottage, ready to suck away their life as soon as they crossed the threshold. Home is where the vacuum is. "Could we sleep here? On the floor somewhere?"

Stils reached under the bar. "Catch." They threw over a couple of old wool blankets and an unclean pillow with feathers poking through.

Syns gave thanks and made a bed in the corner near the blackened hearth.

The Loading Dock

SMELL OF WOODSMOKE, scratch of blanket.

Syns lay watching dust motes drifting in a shaft of sunlight. They pursed their lips and blew upwards; the motes rose, trembled, and began their graceful descent again.

We were in love yesterday. Are we still? Poking around like a tongue for a toothache. Yes. Are we miserable? Poke poke. No!

Warmth and hope suffused the body. A better morning than any they could recall. Admittedly, large tracts of brain functioning were absent. For example, any understanding of causality or of relationships between things. They simply *were*. In love. It were done. Fear and anxiety had passed on like a storm front.

Stils entered. "You're awake. Breakfast?"

Syns pushed aside the blankets and stood. Moderate reeling. "Mmm, no."

"Hair of the dog?"

"No thank you." They walked to the bar, leaves and dirt falling.

Stils went through a door next to the bar. After awhile they came out carrying breakfast. "You free today?"

Are we free? There's the book. A meteor appeared from nowhere, aiming straight for Syns' head. Their hands shook. "On second thought, about the dog hair, we'll take the whole pelt."

Stils pulled a pint of Old Usual. "Wondered if you

might like to come down to the loading dock and help us pick up the new barrels."

"Yeah. About breakfast . . ."

It was companionable eating with Stils, occasionally picking out the odd leaf that fell, like a harbinger of autumn, onto the scrambled eggs.

They were down at the main loading dock in New N, hoisting barrels from the delivery truck and putting them onto an ox-drawn wagon, the principal method of distribution for M. The air was heavy but clear, Syns' muscles were weak but willing, and Stils were cheerful but quiet.

"We've been thinking about your advice about taking action. Any suggestions?"

"Pursue. Try to become lovers."

"Jees."

"Find a way."

The methodology was vague but encouraging. On this glorious morning their heart were ready to love anew. Pursue! But how, but how?

Lost

THEY HAD RETURNED TO THE BUTTS and unloaded the barrels. Now they were relaxing with quick pints and ham sandwiches.

"We'll be taking off for a couple of days," said Stils. "Back on Saturday around noon, reopen at three. You're welcome to stay. Eat and drink anything you want."

Syns had forgotten that after a tournament M closed down. They were disappointed that Stils were leaving but the alehouse was still better than home.

They decided to take a walk. The feet wandered where they would while the mind pondered the riddle "Try to become lovers." They were all for it but—how?

Their mood sank. Lower unto despair and lower still. Though the sun continued to shine, all color was leached away, along with shadow, depth, every interest to the eye. A white dust hung in the air. Everything was flat, empty, desiccated.

What did the barkeep know? Nothing but platitudes. Try to become lovers forsooth! Reality was unhelpful at best, hostile at worst. What was the point of foolish action toward certain failure?

They passed some H's who were laughing shrilly.

This near-insanity emanates from ourselves. Who could love such a person? For us the attainment of love could only be by deceit. If we gain the lover we pity them. If they do not flee we flee instead, to prevent them from throwing their life away on our unworthiness.

Superimposed on this bleached world, the vision of the turn, over and over, trente-deux fouettés en tournant.

They walked up the high road past the shops, tournament grounds, castle, cathedral, knight school, practice field, stables, and outbuildings, to the pasture at the far end of M. They sat on a hillock and gazed back across the town.

Rels came out of the castle and looked to left and right. Seeing us, they turned and approached, smiling sadly. "May we sit beside you?"

We nodded.

"We are glad to find you here." They sat down next to us. "We have been wanting to speak with you. You know what it are concerning. Look at us."

We turned our head, looked into perfect eyes in a perfect face.

"We know you love us."

We blinked.

"And we are . . . grateful."

A lump was forming in our throat. Tears were gathering behind our eyes.

"But we do not, we cannot love you, we cannot be with you."

Tears rolled down our face. We turned away.

"Look at us again."

Reluctantly we turned back.

"It are not wrong that you love us. We are sad for your

sorrow, we are honored by your love."

Tears gushed so hard we could no longer see the perfect face so near. The Sovereign embraced us. We felt their heart beating.

We nodded, unable to speak for grief. Knowing that this was the only touch we would ever have from the perfect being. The only conversation. The only time.

"We must go now. Be not troubled. You will find another."

"Never," we whispered, watching them go, away, away from us, disappearing into the distance.

Syns were bent forward, sobbing.

Time passed. They sat up and looked at the castle. Why do we have these fantasies? Since childhood, fantasies like this. Practicing for failure. Why can't we have fantasies of love going well? Other people do, one hear. Perhaps that is the first action, to try to have better fantasies.

They stood and walked along the back fence behind the sheep-grazing area. The sky was blue again; their tears had washed away the white dust. Maybe that was the function of the sad fantasies, to bring back the beauty of the world. Could a happy fantasy do it too?

Butter and Rain

DISTANT THUNDER, A SUDDEN COOLING of the air. Syns raced to the Butts. Rain began midway. When we get back we will light a fire, have a pint, make a good dinner.

They closed the door and tore off their clothes; muddy rivulets coursed down their body. They dried off with a bar towel. They wrapped themselves in an apron, put on a leathern tunic, which hung on pegs on the wall. Behind the bar they found a pair of stretched-out shoes, slipped into them. They drew a pint.

They went through the door next to the bar and were in a large kitchen. Interior shutters blocked the window. Syns opened them and watched the rain as gray light deepened into evening.

Off the kitchen hummed a walk-in refrigerator. Syns walked in. They examined the loaded shelves, then picked up a loaf of bread and an unopened five-pound brick of butter. In the kitchen was a prep area with a long cutting board. Beside it were various appliances. Syns cut a slice of bread and put it in the toaster.

Heavenly toast. When it was finger-burning hot they popped it out and spread on some butter. They took a bite. Impossible to eat without the vocal cords vibrating through closed lips.

There were no thoughts as they ate and watched the rain, only sensations of pleasure. When they were finished they made another piece of toast, putting the butter

on more thickly. One thought did flicker past: they hadn't
eaten butter in years, normally they didn't even like it.

They sliced off a sliver of butter and ate that. They
watched the rain and sipped ale. They cleaned the board
and sealed up the food and put it back into the refrigerator.
They walked out into the pub. It was dark and chilly.
They went back into the kitchen. Was this only the second
night since the turn?

They took out the bread and butter again. They made
more buttered toast, followed by thin slices of butter from
the blade of the knife. All the while watching rain and
darkness. The world was intoxicatingly lovely.

They brought their blankets and pillow into the kitchen
and slept with the smell of toast.

The following morning it was still raining. Syns ate buttered toast and looked out the window. They ate slices of
butter. Once in awhile they sipped at a pint of Usual.

They had done this once before, gone into a trance of
eating. They'd been alone then too. Sourdough bread and
butter and white wine. Pleasurable but disconcerting. A
few days later it was over.

They'd never expected to revisit that time. They had
assumed that they'd become, if not wiser, at least more
capable of a disciplined life. Now the intervening years
seemed but a detour; they were back on the main road and
hadn't changed at all.

Syns cut a thin slice of butter with a long sharp knife.
Put it into their mouth. Looked out at the rain. There was

nothing in the world they would rather be doing.

A whole day passed. The next morning their lungs were inflated with anxiety, the awareness that Stils would be returning in a few hours. It seemed essential to remove every trace of what they had done. They dressed in their brittle clothes and went out.

The rain had stopped. On the ground were bright puddles and orphaned leaves.

Syns walked swiftly to F-town's liquor store, the Flying Highball. It carried additional necessities. They bought four quarter-pound sticks of butter.

They hurried back. With a wide knife they formed the butter onto the brick like a sculptor in clay, wrapped and sealed it and returned it to its spot in the refrigerator. They repositioned the bread loaves to hide the fact that one was missing, took the toaster outside and emptied it, cleaned every crumb from the counter, swept the floor, closed the shutters, set the blankets and pillow beside the hearth, put the shoes behind the bar, and hung the apron and tunic on their pegs.

Stils returned at noon.

Syns were seated at the bar nursing a pint. They were back in the world where they didn't like butter, and fish and fries at the JetFish was the best imaginable dinner.

Pursuant

LIGHTHEARDED UNTO GIDDINESS to have company again, Syns chatted with Stils. The barkeep made sandwiches and tested the taps.

At three the doors reopened. A few regulars came in and gradually the place filled. Syns were content to sit and drink, joining the desultory conversation. In the evening their eyes were closing. Stils said, "You know, there's room in the kitchen if you want to turn in early."

They fell into a deep sleep, to the hum of the refrigerator and the low rumble from the bar.

The next day they were up early. They felt like taking another walk.

"Syns?"

It was late in the day and our hero were near the entrance gate. They turned and beheld a stranger.

"Syns? Are that you? We can't believe it! We've been looking all over for you. We're a huge fan. Would you sign our book?" The stranger were holding out a pen and *The Double Jewels*.

"Yes, of course. How do you spell your name?"

"B-L-A-T-S."

Syns wrote briefly and handed back the book.

Blats looked eagerly at the inscription. Their face fell. "Oh."

"Are something wrong?"

"Oh, no. No."

"Okay then, nice meeting you."

"Wait, where are you going?"

Syns felt a finger of dread poke sharply at their chest. "Now? Actually we have to meet someone."

"You can't. We're your biggest fan. We're . . ." the fan paused. With steady gaze and clear voice they continued, " . . . in love with you."

"Oh, well, if you knew us better, your . . . idea would vanish."

"We *knew* you were going to say that. We know you so well. We've been looking for you. Waiting for you. Waiting and waiting by your cottage."

"Well, you know, we're sorry." Syns were backing away.

"Wh—when will we see each other again?"

"Maybe our next book signing?"

"Just *us*. Alone. We're meant to be together."

"We really don't think—"

"You *have* to! We've been waiting—"

Syns were running toward the Butts yelling, "Sorry, sorry."

They dashed into the kitchen. Later they came out.

"What was that all about?" asked Stils.

"Nothing. Shot please."

But even after a couple of drinks Syns were too nervous to remain so exposed. They went back into the kitchen, disturbed unto forgetting their love.

They slept all night. When they awoke, the turn was in their eyes and their libido were back, frightening in its intensity. Love were so brutal; behind the flying monkeys of the psyche loomed the great demon reality. How did humans do it?—fall in love not knowing what the other would do: hurt them unbearably, or . . . possibly not.

After breakfast they went out into the hot late-summer morning with the idea of being more adventurous. They had to devise a plan not only for love but for life.

They started along the path toward their cottage where slumbered their half-remembered belongings, their half-forgotten manuscript.

Divestiture

GREEN SWORDS ON THE GREENSWARD, romance number seventeen. The very title made Syns wince. At the door of their cottage they froze.

In M and F-town you could look fairly odd without raising much notice. Not so in the Normals where conventionality was prized, especially in Old N. There were stares from those Syns passed—out walking dogs, carrying bags of groceries and golf clubs, weeding, bicycling, walking in groups with picnic baskets. One rain-shower was Syns' only cleansing for days; dirt and a few small leaves still fell from their hair.

They proceeded past the duck pond, the tennis courts, and the putting green, to the little shopping mall where Frits their agent had an office next to a bowling alley.

A bell sounded as they came through the glass door. Frits' assistant Rhys looked up, frowning through heavy-rimmed glasses.

"Syns! For heavens' sakes, we barely recognized you. Are you ill?"

"Hullo, Rhys. In a manner of speaking. Frits in?"

"Where else would they be?"

Syns opened a door. "Frits, it're us."

A voice came from behind a stack of manuscripts. "Syns? That you? Come on back."

Syns rounded the stack.

Frits were standing with yet another manuscript in

hand. "You look terrible! What happened?"

"We, uh . . ."

"You want a drink?"

"No thanks. Ah, we have to stop writing."

"What is it? Tell us." There was obvious concern in Frits' harsh voice.

"It's just . . . we have to take some time off."

"Well, gods know you deserve it. And obviously you need it. We'll take care of everything. But you'll have to see the Mayor and Gots yourselves. Have you seen a doctor?"

"Nah."

"Can you give us an estim—"

"No."

"Okay. Anything else? Sure you don't want to talk about it?"

"No thanks."

"Rest up. Take a vacation."

"Yeh, we'll think about it." The Mayor. They hadn't considered a stop-work release, having never stopped before.

The true Mayor of H-town and all administration, aside from some functions still done in the barracks, were in Old N. The Mayor of M were a ceremonial position. F and New N didn't even have them.

Syns walked downtown. City Hall was the most impressive of many two-story buildings—red-brick with a tall white-columned portico.

Syns were ushered into the presence of the Mayor. They'd never met, but each were famous in their own way.

"Syns! Well, well, well. It're a pleasure!" The Mayor had big rows of blinding teeth and a mighty, two-handed shake. They were the first person in Old N who didn't seem alarmed at Syns' appearance. "What can we do for you?"

"Frits our agent said we needed a work stop permit."

"Taking a break, huh? Say, that last book—what was it?—*Ardor in Armor*, terrific, terrific."

"Thanks. Yeh, we need a break."

"Okey dokey. How long you want it for?"

"See, that's just it. We don't know."

"Got a ballpark?"

"Not really."

"You feeling under the weather?"

"Possibly."

"Say, real sorry to hear that. Go on over to the hospital and let 'em take a look-see."

"Yeh."

The Mayor signed a form and handed a carbon copy to Syns. "Okay then, you take good care now, ya' hear?"

"Thanks."

"Not at all, not at all." The Mayor gave another jackhammer handshake in parting.

In New N, buildings tended toward glass-and-steel severity, somewhat miniaturized. H-Town Publishing dominated them all. The lobby attendant recognized Syns and sent them up. Syns took the elevator.

Gots had a big corner office in ceiling-to-floor glass, ficus plants, a giant empty-topped desk, wall-to-wall carpeting in charcoal gray, and photos of H-town's most successful authors on the interior walls. Syns were there, looking so young and earnest it were painful. Gots took one look at Syns and rushed over, arms outstretched as if to catch them if they fell. "Sit down. You need some water?"

"No thanks, we're fine."

"Whatever you say. Business or social? As if you ever did social."

"Yeh, it's business. Frits said we should see you in person about taking some time off."

"Time off? You? Are you ill? Dying? Having a nervous breakdown?"

"Maybe all three."

"That's terrible. What can we do? Anything."

"We need indefinite time off. We got the stop-work permit."

"Well, of course." Gots looked at Syns with troubled eyes. "As friends, are you going to make it?"

"We think so. We hope so. Don't worry too much. It's not a deadly disease or anything." Or was it?

"You want to stay in the penthouse for awhile? Great guest-room. View, whirlpool, quiet, especially after hours."

"Thanks. Really. But no. We have some things we've got to do."

"You're not leaving H-town are you?"

"Of course not."

"Don't mean to pry but are you, ah, having writer's block? Because they have workshops—"

"No!"

"Okay, okay."

"Look, we don't know. Something having to do with hatred. Writer's hatred."

"Sounds terrible. Never heard of a workshop for that."

"We don't need a workshop. We just have to stop for awhile."

"Alright. We'll put everything on hold for *Green Swords*. Gots paused. "You want to have dinner sometime?"

"We don't know. Really. We'll let you know."

The publisher looked distressed. "Don't forget to eat. You have somebody to look after you?"

"Yeh. Listen, we have to go now."

"Okay. Go to a spa. Get a massage. Take it easy. Forget completely about the book."

Syns, already exiting, shouted back, "Thanks, really." Too impatient to wait for the elevator, they ran down the stairs in a frenzy.

Freedom!

They were back in M. We have liberated all our time. Now what? They wandered lost again.

Very late, they returned to the Butts. The clientele had gone home and Stils were sweeping up.

"Can we talk?"

"Shoot."

"We divested of the book. We're on a sort of medical leave. For what it's worth."

"Excellent."

"It doesn't feel that way. We could not be writing at present, or perhaps ever again. But other than that, nothing has changed."

"It was a wise thing to do."

"There's something else."

Stils kept sweeping.

"It happened yesterday." Syns related the meeting with the fan.

"Why is that so bad?"

"Because—don't you see?—that're what *we* are, an obsessed fan."

"You're too hard on yourselves. The circumstances are not the same."

Telling the barkeep about the fan made it unbearably clear that the circumstances were exactly the same.

Overcome, they fled into the night.

Stepping Out and Into

Syns ran toward the castle and beyond. When they came to the knights' training ground they climbed over the fence and walked onto the field.

Something soft and fragrant affixed itself to their shoe. Where to scrape it off? A hay bale. Probably some were near the stables, a darker shadow against the sky.

"Whatch'er doin'?"

"Jees!" Syns jumped in fright. "Stepped into some horse-shit if you must know. Looking for a place to scrape it off."

"But whatch'er doin' *here*?"

"Trying to figure out our lives."

"Huh. What happened? Lost yer job?"

Syns paused. "Uh, yes, in fact."

"That it? Yer lookin' for work?"

"Perhaps we are."

"Ther's a job here. Somebody quit today. Not every-body's cup o' punch."

"Doing what?"

"Muckin'."

Horses. Simple, honest, horses. "We want it. We have to have it."

"Come back tomorrow."

"We want it now."

"Yer crazy?"

"Where do we apply?"

"Head groom. Tomorrow."

"Where are they now?"

"Where else? In ther room sleepin' off a binge."

"Take us."

"Yer definitely crazy," laughed the voice. But they left them at the head groom's door. "Yer own funeral."

Syns knocked with increasing vigor.

Eventually the door opened. "What the *fucks*?!"

"We want the job. We must have the job."

"Come back tomorrow."

"We must have it now, tonight."

"What're your name?"

Syns were nothing if not inventive. "Akas."

"It's yours. Show up at seven in the morning. Now get the hells out of here."

"We need a place to stay."

After further wrangling, Syns were taken to a bed in the muckers' dormitory. The room was ripe with snoring, snorting, belching, and farting. Syns crawled under the rough blanket.

Action has been taken. Our old life are over. We are a mucker now. Perhaps it will be a calamity. Perhaps it is a clear sign that we are mad.

But in truth they felt better. They felt excited, wondering what this new life would bring.

Aegean Rhapsody

AMID SOUNDS OF CURSING, coughing, and hacking, Syns were awakened, along with the rest of the muckers.

During the hearty breakfast in the dining hall almost everyone smoked and many gulped tankards of ale. Then off they went to the stables. The grooms had already taken the horses out to the field. The muckers cleaned the stalls, tossed and banked the hay. It was companionable, joking together in the slats of sunlight cutting in between the warped boards. Mucking was a straightforward enterprise.

For Syns, unaccustomed to it, the work was blistering, backbreaking, and likeable. We were meant for physical tasks. No paragraphs, no grammar, no lies.

After awhile the grooms led the horses into the stables and the muckers went into the field, where they mucked a bit, filled in divots, and looked for other threats to hooves.

Next came lunch, another ample affair. When they returned to the field the young knights were there, some in armor, some still in beginners' leather. Grooms and muckers assisted, handling lances and shields, righting the quintain, hanging the rings, refastening armor, running errands, and otherwise loafing and smoking. By midafternoon the grooms had slipped away. They muckers stayed on until it was time to wash up for dinner.

The communal shower was Syns' first in countless days. They were amazed; the water coursing down their body ran almost black. Everyone dressed and headed for the pub. The muckers had their own, the Horses' Asses, next to the dining hall. Winking and laughing, they asked Akas what had happened at their last job that necessitated a change in the middle of the night. Syns laughed and rolled their eyes.

Another source of merriment was Akas' clothing, derelict even by mucker standards. Some extra garments were donated in return for a round of drinks from their first paycheck. In short, Akas were accepted.

Dinner was taken in the pub. Afterwards some played cards or draughts, almost all continued to drink. Syns dragged themselves upstairs and keeled over into bed.

As they were falling asleep, a vision: the room was cold and Rels were there. Rels suggested sleeping next to each other to keep warm. They crawled into bed, fully clothed. Rels embraced the length of Syns' body from the back. Syns felt their breathing, warmth, the pressure of their body . . .

They awoke with blistered hands, burning arms, a sore back, and a hangover. They felt good.

They skipped breakfast and joined the rest of the muckers as they headed toward the stables in the pure blue of a summer morning.

Amid the routine of their labors Syns had time to think. The world was so beautiful it helped to have a lover to contain the intensity of it. Their happiness at being with the muckers increased their desire until it became its own darkness.

Syns realized that for them everything was painful; it was their orientation to life. Nonetheless, some forms of pain were better than others. For example, the pain now was better than before the turn.

A set of points on a graph through which various curves can be drawn: one through the low points, one through the high, one connecting them all. Thus your life, depending on which way you interpret the data. If you can, draw your curve through the high points and call it reality.

Autonomy. We say we want it but we construct our lives to insure against it. Because on a difficult day the bondage of obligation is what saves us from our troubled will. Society exist for this purpose. Syns felt gratitude for the demands of the job: to rise, to work, to fit in.

Goals: to minimize shame and pessimism. To eschew wallowing. To contain impulsiveness when negativity ruled. To be patient. To look down the longer road rather than at the cobblestones beneath the feet. To imagine success.

In the late afternoon the head mucker, Hercs, asked Akas it they would like to learn how to groom a horse. Syns were agreeable. They went into the stables.

Hercs said, "Akas, this are Whooshes, a new arrival. One of the finest horses we have seen."

Syns were taught to wipe down, pick out, curry, check for various injuries and diseases. And to listen, to speak, to touch with sureness and tenderness.

And the morning and the evening were the second day at the muckers. It was already home.

At bedtime, surrounded by breathing bodies, Syns were abraded by loneliness and longing. Falling in love had stripped away so much. Being with the muckers revealed the necessity of what they now possessed: the presence of others for survival itself.

Dreams. Bits, windows. A friend who, learning of Syns' love, set out to steal Rels away, and succeeded. Waking, seeking to understand the dream. A warning? The muckers knew nothing of Syns' desire. The secret was buried deeper than at the barkeep's; perhaps this retreat had been necessary.

Tears came often, falling on the hay in the stables, the grass in the field.

Love ebbed and flowed like the tides, in great fluxions like the Bay of Fundy. Syns would lose touch with thoughts of Rels, then love rushed back in.

The ridge of love. At times you are undone because you feel so much, at other times because you feel so little. In between, a knife-sharp ridge. You must make an effort not to fall into the abyss on either side. Sometimes the best you can do is oscillate in shimmering uncertainty.

At times Syns were happy about their pursuit of Rels. They even took pride in the foolhardiness of their ambition.

Overall they felt like the horses, a numbish endurance. They worked so hard, were so physically tired, the pain were not too deep most of the time.

They went out for an evening stroll in the field, the front yard of their new home. Stars, the scents of dry grass and green leaf. A musician were practicing the sackbut. Syns had the absolute sensation of dancing with Rels. Like a blow to the midsection it knocked the wind out of them; they hunched forward in surprise. The musician strolled on.

An idea arced across the sky: they would become a knight; they would become the best knight in all the land.

What luck that they had stumbled into the mucking life. Without it they might never have found their way.

They felt something new. Could it be hope? Perhaps it was lunacy. Perhaps there was no difference.

They had not only entered the casino of bad odds, they had sat down to play. You hold the cards you were dealt whether your hands shake or no. Good cards and bad, win and lose. If you sit at the table your chances go from zero to infinitesimal. That is called progress.

After the musician, after the illumination, Syns went to the Asses where the muckers were carousing as usual. Someone were saying, "Maybe we should become a knight and hope they don't notice." It sent a chill through Syns' heart. But they joined in the laughter at such absurdity.

They dreamed again that night.

Sometimes you wake up from a deep sleep and you have been dreaming of the lover's body, it have come to inhabit your own. And not just the body, the entire being of the other are within you. This phenomenon, perhaps, is one of the things that guides the choice of a lover. So that on those mornings you wake up more comforted than troubled, more found than lost, feeling that something wonderful has happened.

Hieratics I
The Young Knights

SYNS SAID NOTHING OF THEIR PLAN but they began to watch the young knights with a keener eye. Except for the children's school still maintained at Visitors, the knights-in-training were the youngest group in H-town. One could enroll at fifteen. Every one of them were a tall.

This single exception to the equality law had occurred because so many people wanted to be knights and because it required so much training and expense. It was impossible to allow everyone who desired knighthood to attain it. A lottery was attempted but there were still endless disputes. The restriction to talls led to a lot of grumbling but eventually things settled down.

The knights knew they were one of the principal attractions of H-town and displayed a subtle air of superiority. Though they received equal H-town wages they lived somewhat outside the rules. All gifts were supposed to be equally distributed. The knights did not always comply and no one did anything about it. Those from wealthy families often brought their own horses and armor and probably other things no one knew about. Unless they became unfit they did not have to change jobs.

They were the gods of H-town. They were not overtly condescending, they simply did not pay much attention to those they considered beneath them.

Hieratics II
Muckers and Grooms

EVERY SOCIETY HAVE ITS PECKING ORDER and the stables and training ground of Old M were no exception.

To the uninformed the grooms were of a higher order than the muckers because their care of the horses appeared, at first blush, to be loftier than what the muckers did.

The head groom, Frangs, were of this mind. They were the overseer of both grooms and muckers, whilst the head mucker, Hercs, were only in charge of the muckers. Frangs were a shirker and a snob. They felt that the less they worked the more prestigious their standing. The other grooms were encouraged to feel the same way.

Not so, Hercs. They loved both their work and the horses. They were always around the field and stables when they weren't at the Asses. Furthermore, they were a brilliant trainer of both horses and riders, and over time these jobs became theirs. The other muckers tended to take after Hercs. Minimal work was not the goal, enjoying both work and recreation was.

The grooms were expected to see to each horse in the morning and assist the knights in the afternoon. After training, the knights were supposed to pick out and groom their horses themselves. But in truth some knights were lazy. It had developed that for a nominal fee they could get someone to do it for them. The grooms were no longer around when training was over. The muckers were happy to oblige.

That was how it had come to pass that Whooshes were groomed by Syns. They belonged to Ayrds, the newest, youngest, and wealthiest knight-in-training. Whooshes were a beautiful black hermaphrodite with a perfectly symmetrical blaze, spirited, strong, and of an unusually sweet disposition.

Knight Train

SYNS, MOUNTED ON WHOOSHES, took a wild swing at the quintain, missing it completely.

"O ye aren the fairest of knights!" shouted the wag Els, joined in laughter by the other muckers.

Undaunted, they circled around for another tilt. Hercs admonished, "Don't look at your lance at all. Look at the quintain, don't look away for even a moment."

Early evening in the practice field. Sweet herb smell of grassy turf. Warm air added to the warmth of Whooshes against legs and butt, the breeze of movement cooling perspiration. A faint scent of leather from the tack, perhaps the best scent there is. Soreness, wrist to shoulder, from holding the ashen spear. The drum of hooves.

The faces of friends looking up, smiling. Hercs ahead, next to the quintain, unblinking.

Only the wooden figure now. Nothing else—not sky nor ground nor horse nor lance nor friend nor teacher—only the figure growing larger with each hoofbeat.

A sharp strike! Glancing over at Hercs.

A mighty blow upon the back. Unseated, stricken upon the unforgiving ground. Stars, all in a swath like the Milky Way.

Loud hoots of laughter.

When breath comes, we laugh too. The strike was off-center, the figure doles its punishment. Pain throbs but the heart are joyous.

Later at the bar Syns impetuously revealed their plan—not about Rels, but that they were serious about becoming a knight. Impulse: the final result of long-deliberated action. Everyone loved the joke and declared their willingness to help. "You are a funny dirty crazy clown but harmless."

"We are sincere. The first thing we are going to do is quit drinking." And they did.

In bed that night Syns thought about the fact that for once they were taking action specifically motivated by love. It brought to mind an infatuation from back in their smithy days. Bims were someone famous they did not know, who lived far away. By a twist of fate Bims learned of Syns through a mutual acquaintance. Syns never told a soul of their infatuation. But once, when Syns were in Visitors talking on the phone to the mutual acquaintance, they heard Bims laughing in the background. Bims grabbed the phone and suggested that Syns come to visit and get drunk with them. Not only did Syns not go, the thought of doing so never occurred to them.

The transformation of the imaginary into the real. Time will pass and something will happen, one way or another. Even if nothing happens, that is something. It will be reality, it will be truth.

The biggest problem of action is the inexorable increase in anxiety, as you await the transformation of the vague unblemished future into the specific pockmarked present.

The greatest fear? That despite your best efforts, and even if your actions were somehow adequate, the timing would be wrong. This allemande, this shifting of the stage set—so many actors, doors opening and closing; you go to the proscenium when you can and take your chance. It is the only entrance to love, though your moment is, at best, the blink of the blink of an eye.

In addition to the trainees, the older knights came by to practice, bringing their squires. Cyras the Giant were among them. Syns assessed the competition. Yet how could they be competition when they were of a different species altogether? Syns fantasized killing off all the knights. Most surely their blood on the ground, like dragons' teeth, would only sprout new rivals.

Syns could no longer live with themselves unless they pursued. Were they not to act, something defining and unacceptable would happen.

Their armor of cynicism was wrenched away as they entered the melee of imperatives. Should they fail, the effort was still necessary, though they could not help thinking, O, it may altogether break our heart, the worst suffering of this lifetime.

You look down the road that vanishes into the blue-gray distance, your future. In actuality your destiny is more likely to be the little rocky path that appears suddenly and heads off at a right angle.

Cycles to the days: mornings tended to be good, middays bad, late afternoons and evenings good, nights bad.

So much physical work, such a different life. No hatred anymore. The muckers joked about Akas trying to win Rels, having no idea what lay in their heart. Syns joked back. In the night they wept for desire.

The effect of action on the malady of love: it is therapeutic. For one thing, passivity itself is discouraging. For another, moving muscles in the light of day inevitably summons the squabbling family, reality. Gone is the tedium of contemplation. Reality's irritations, demands, and especially its limitations, bring a particular relief. As for the future—good comes of bad, bad comes of good, truth comes in time.

The more pleasurable something is, the easier it is to let it go. Pleasure has already rewarded you. It is when something is painful that you hate to give it up; you want to make your suffering worth something. It's so hard to push away from the gambling table when you are losing. Therefore try to enjoy love as much as possible, to suffer as little as possible. So that, among other things, you can give it up if you must.

When Syns were younger and love were successful they felt disoriented and looked for a way out.

Would the Sovereign be all we had hoped for, all we had imagined? There are only two requirements of a soulmate: first, they must spark the fantasy of complete accord; second, they must make good on the fantasy. But what is the meaning of soulmate anyway, when we ourselves are so flawed?

What if Rels *were* faultless and by a miracle we got together. Then might not Rels change? You can never be safe. If Rels changed for the worse would we stay or go? We have no idea. But for once we would try as hard as we could to stay.

Love seem forever. It so rarely are. But still, this cannot be a deterrent before it happen, should it happen.

Syns wondered what it was about the turn that had captured them so completely. Something familiar and yet not. Even if what were to attract you was the fact that the other *cannot love*, you must do as love command.

They could not avoid thinking about the possibility that they might be the one to grow dissatisfied with Rels. Then Rels would grow dissatisfied with their dissatisfaction. Passion can subside even if it do not vanish entirely. Courage when love are strong, when love are weak.

And the ultimate fantasy: that love would perfect us all. One more vestige of a lifetime of bad habits.

Stealth and Shock

THE EIGHTH DAY OF SYNS' TRAINING went well. They hit the quintain every time, spinning it as skillfully as Cyras, and didn't miss a ring.

"Now if only ye could grow a foot," quipped Els.

"That's our next project."

They groomed Whooshes, showered, and repaired to the pub with the gang. They were too nervous to eat but no one noticed. As everyone slid deeper into their cups, Syns went outside.

They were not certain if the heaviness in the air was meteorological or a reflection of their inner state. They made their way to the stables, to Whooshes, carrying apple and oat. "Buddies, this is it."

The horse armor was kept in a special room. Whooshes' had arrived recently. Hercs and Syns had started the process of familiarizing the horse with its weight and feel.

Syns led them, in full tack, into the armoring room and attached shaffron, crinet, petral, flanchards, and crupper, as well as saddle steels. Fully barded, the horse were magnificent. Syns grabbed a lance by the butt, mounted, and rode through the door to the high road, then the short way down to the knight school. Tying the lead to a tree, Syns proffered an apple, saying, "Wait here, buddies, we'll be right back."

They'd been to the school a few times, running errands. The entry hall was empty. Laughter and clanging silverware reverberated from the refectory.

They went up the staircase and along a hallway. The knights' nameplates were on the doors. They found Ayrds' and entered; the room was illuminated only by the sconces in the hallway. How easy reality was to deal with if you were brave. Exert will and reality gave way.

Syns lit the lantern on the bedside table and gasped. Every inch of wall and ceiling was covered with pictures—of Rels.

Knees trembling, they sank onto the bed. We are too late. All our efforts and plans have been in vain. And even if . . . it . . . have not yet come to pass, it will.

Was every room plastered with such pictures? Were every knight in love with the Sovereign? And why not? One of them *would* be their next lover. Not a pathetic writer turned mucker turned thief. Syns felt a sickening wave of pure selves-hatred.

Curiosity got the better of them. They examined every photograph, feeling more deeply in love, more deeply in despair, at every moment. Rels looking surprised, bored, amused, angry, in close up and long shot, alone and surrounded by their court. In a framed photo by the bedside the Sovereign stood next to a grinning Ayrds.

Where had the photos come from? Did Rels have their own photographer following after them? Next to the prize photo was a magazine, Sovereign Secrets. Syns leafed through it. Reports of sightings and gossip. Candid pics. On the back were listed times for Rels' fan club meetings, held at the dance pavilion. Ye gods. The place was enormous.

A flare of lightning, a rumble of thunder. The excited chatter of objects struck by raindrops.

Ayrds had been bragging about their new armor, which had arrived a few days before. On the floor a large box was torn open. Syns looked inside. Something gleamed amidst the packing materials.

Ah hells. They harnessed themselves in steel inlaid with silver: sabatons and spurs, greaves, poleyns, cuisses, breastplate and backplate, belt with dagger and scabbard and sword, rerebraces, vambraces, helmet, gauntlets. They picked up the small shield. They snuffed out the lantern and crept, as quietly as they could, down the stairs.

Outside, a downpour, turning dusty earth into slick mud. They skidded and slid to a nervous Whooshes.

The rain was blinding. Added to that, Syns could barely see through the helmet's visor. After many attempts they succeeded in mounting their trusty steed.

And now, at last, for adventure, heigh-ho!

Book Two: Errant

Sacred Matters

OFF THEY WENT for about fifteen yards. Whooshes splashed into a puddle and slipped; Syns tumbled off into water and mud. Any lingering dismay over the photos was unseated by acute misery: a hard landing and cold wet muddy armor.

Another clash of lightning and thunder. Whooshes shrieked.

They were nearest the cathedral. Syns led the horse up the front steps to the porch and threw open the arched doors. They went in.

They crossed the vestibule and entered the nave. Votives trembled on the altar. Kriks had done a magnificent job, conveying gothic grandeur despite the modest scale. Columns and shafts disappeared into vaulted dimness.

Syns ran ahead, tearing off armor and clothing as they went. They stepped up to the chancel. They shoved the candles aside and grabbed an altar cloth. Returning to Whooshes, they removed their horse-armor and padding and commenced to rub them down. The horse quieted. The cloth was soon dripping. Syns took another from the altar, and another. After a thorough drying, picking out, feeding and watering, Syns made a stall between the pews with wadded up pages torn from hymnals. Whooshes promptly went to sleep. Syns had dried off during the exertion. They tucked a white cloth around their waist and flung another over their shoulders.

Our hero had been sober for several days. They now wished to make a change. On intuition they went up into the pulpit. In a deep drawer were several bibles, prayer books, missals, and old bulletins. Moving them aside exposed a nearly full bottle of cheap port.

Syns hated the stuff but in a storm you could not be choosy. They took a few swigs, wincing. It got easier after that. By the time they had gulped down a quarter of the bottle they felt warmed and redeemed.

Also intensely hungry. A search produced nothing but a tin of communion wafers. They poked their head out the front doors in hope of inspiration.

A flash of lightning. A dark shape thumped onto the steps. Syns threw off their wraps and went out to see what it was.

A wild goose. They touched it. Warm but deceased. Syns had written about cooking a goose many times but had omitted the graphic stages of preparation, of which they were ignorant. They didn't even know what kind of goose this was, though at least it seemed young and healthy. Despite the port they felt a bit frightened. But they were famished and this was their new brave life.

They plucked off the feathers and brought it inside. They broke up one of the wooden tables near the entrance. Using bulletins and missals for kindling, they started a fire. They lit a taper from the altar and singed off the down and pinfeathers. They grabbed their dagger and the bird and went back out into the rain. Now for the hardest part: they cut a slit from breastbone to vent and reached in. Zounds what warmth. They grabbed whatever innards they could and yanked them out. They laid the bird down on a step and decapitated it. Had to be done. They washed it inside and out in the rain and it finally started to cool down. Syns were shivering. They felt around and grabbed a few more innards and when the cavity seemed pretty much empty they washed it again and their own hands and arms. They returned to the vestibule and dried the bird carefully. On a wooden table was a font, a small marble basin with a little holy water in it. They dumped out the water and used the basin to make some stuffing: a little port, some crumbled wafers, and one of Whooshes' apples, cut up. They stuffed the bird. They poked holes in the skin along the cavity with their dagger. They trussed it together with ribbons from prayer books. They tied the wings and legs up with more ribbons. They started to feel calmer, finally. The fire had burned down to some respectable coals.

Above the altar was, among other icons, a good-sized metal crucifix. They climbed up and yanked at the foot of it and after awhile it came down. They spitted the bird with the crucifix's long leg. They brought two tables near the coals, one at either side. They rested opposites ends of the crucifix on the tables in such a way that the crucified bird was above the coals in the space between the tables. They put the font underneath to catch the drippings.

They drank some more port. They cleaned all the

armor while their clothing and Whooshes' padding steamed near the fire. Soon the transubstantiational smell of roasting fowl filled the church. Fat was melting off and sizzling. They turned the bird and basted it using a long-handled candle snuffer for a ladle. They opened the doors a little to make sure they didn't die of smoke inhalation.

When the goose was done they laid it to cool on an offertory plate and when it could be handled they sat on the floor near the fire and devoured it, grease sliding down to their elbows, resurrected by pleasure.

They were in a cathedral, fed, clean, and wearing white. "Well, why the hells not?"

The altar went up several levels on graduated tables. They hauled their armor to the highest one, along with the rest of the port which they poured into a chalice. They clambered up and knelt down.

Phrases came easily, culled from a lifetime of hack writing. "Do ye swear fealty to us, through all hardship and adversity?"

"Yea, our liege."

"Do ye swear to acts of bravery and courage against all odds?"

"Yea, our liege."

Vows were interspersed with putting on the armor, blessing each article, with particular attention to the spurs. "Shall ye be hardy, courteous, loyal and of fair speech, ferocious to foes and debonair to friends?"

"Yea, our liege."

Lastly they picked up the sword and held it point down in front of them. "We dub ye . . ." Syns looked down. "Silver Knight. Be ye a knight."

They smacked themselves on the shoulder with the sword. They drained the chalice. "Arise, knight."

They slid down from the altar. They kissed Whooshes.

Subsequent festivities were limited to the chaste dances of the votive flamelets, while our new knight curled up on a pew and slept.

Beautiful Forest

BELLS ANNOUNCED PRIME as pillars of light entered through the rose window and clerestories. It mixed with a smoky haze and found its way to our hero's eyes. They opened. Ye gods it was Sunday. Sugars the priest would be arriving any moment.

Whooshes were already awake. They had relieved themselves healthfully and were eager for the day to begin. Syns barded and mounted their horse and posted to the front doors.

Outside was a crystalline morning. Whooshes avoided the puddles, clip-clopping to the back gate of **M**. A fastening was set high to prevent children from exiting and getting lost. Syns unlatched it and rode through.

Pungent forest scents, enlivened by the storm: needles, cones, fallen and unfallen leaves; florgasms of horsemint and shinleaf. Birds puttered and joked, a light breeze brushed the trees—yet all was immaculately silent and still.

They proceeded to a place by the stream. Syns brushed wet leaves aside, revealing tarps wrapped tightly around the supplies they had been sequestering. The stream, usually apathetic, jumped over the rocks in a saltarello. Dense was the air, dense the shadows. The very light was thick as honey. A density of being in this green world.

Whooshes shivered with elation while Syns groomed and fed them.

The tent was pitched, a campfire lit, coffee and breakfast

prepared. This was the life. The Silver Knight decided to name the forest Arcady.

Gloriously alone, where you can drink and eat and moan with pleasure. Is not the most flaming sunset experienced alone, the most rubious glass of wine? Syns recalled the wild goose and their mouth watered. Ah, the autistic pleasures.

Yet they were not alone, for the good Whooshes were nearby, happily snorting and chewing on tender shoots. After breakfast, horse and rider raced through the forest, in vivid alternations of light and shadow, like an old movie jerking past.

Later, Syns modified their armor for a better fit, filing plates and tightening fastenings. Then jousting practice and lunch.

In the quiet of the outer world, the inner world grew noisier. Here they were, fled into paradise itself, but after all, the unrelenting hounds of their personality had run them to ground.

As the day wore on, our knight grew melancholy. Perhaps they would take a nap. They spent the rest of the day inside the tent; the beauty of the forest had become just a tiny bit oppressive.

Other Forests

Boring

WHAT WERE WE EXPECTING, enchanted castles? Rescuing grateful people in distress? For gods' sakes it's a lousy little forest with scrawny trees and a puny creek already going back to a trickle.

It was the next day and Syns were bored. You simply get tired, at times, of everything. It is physiologic: not enough rest, the aftermath of too much excitement, hangovers worse the second day than the first, not enough to do.

Lonely

Yet another day by the gods damned stream. Syns were starting to feel like they were going out of their mind. For one thing they were lonely. Even in reclusion as a writer there were Livs and Lucs at the library, Stils at the pub. At the muckers they had gotten used to company. How satisfying the simple camaraderie had been.

Are we giving up already? It's only the third morning in the forest. How will we know when it's time to cut our losses?

The memory of Ayrds' wall of photos haunted Syns. *They* had no picture, no relic. Only the prospect of endless days and nights filled with longing and nothingness.

Whooshes came over and nuzzled our knight.

Romance of Romance

At least horses will let you love them. "Thanks, buddies. Not sure you can save us but we appreciate the concern." They leaned their head against the horse's neck and wept.

Night of Dark Doubt

That evening there was a flight into health. No longer feeling in love. Instead, drifting and detachment. The absence of suffering felt like manic happiness.

Then relapsing fever set in. Love and misery increased as the night progressed. What are we *doing?* We are absurd. We couldn't help but laugh if we heard about it.

Cruel fates sat at their looms, weaving the worst moments of Syns' life into a tapestry of failure.

We will survive this night. Tomorrow we surrender. It is over. Syns tucked their sleeping bag tightly around them, covered their head with a pillow, and endured.

The Club

HAVING NOT SLEPT ALL NIGHT, Syns arose early. They tended to Whooshes, then left them at the campground and set out for Old M on foot.

Our knight approached the ballroom in full harness, helmet on, visor down. They were on their way to the seven a.m. meeting of Rels' fan club. Simply, they had run out of ideas.

Others were converging. When Syns saw young Ayrds, not in armor but in an elegant surcoat, their heart squeezed like a concertina.

"Hail," said Ayrds. "Verily, who are you?"

"We are new."

"We thought so. Welcome." Everyone were nodding and greeting each other, shorts and talls from highest to lowest. "Let's go in and get a seat."

"Uh, verily," said Syns. "Could we sit toward the back?"

"Don't be nervous. This is a great meeting. First of the day with all the latest news."

The room was vast, crowded with chairs that were filling rapidly. Ayrds were hailing people, including three young knights Syns recognized. Syns' was the only face obscured.

Our hero were in a state of mild shock: all these people were fans of Rels too. They recognized two regulars from the Butts and other vaguely familiar faces.

"Everyone here are from Old M?"

"O nay, they're from all over H-town, but everyone are required to dress authentically, of course."

Fans beyond M. Hopeless.

A whistle. A stocky goatherd were on the podium. Greetings and murmuring ceased.

"Hail fans of the Sovereign Rels!"

"Hail Rins!"

"We have news!"

Cheers.

"We have a new photo!"

Louder cheers.

"We have a new song!"

Only a few cheers.

"First, any newcomers?"

"Stand up," whispered Ayrds.

Syns stood, heart thrashing around.

"Hail newcomer!" said Rins.

"Uh, Hail!"

Ayrds whispered, "Say who you are. First name only."

What were it? Oh yeah. "Silver Knight."

"Hail Silvers!" shouted the group.

"Do you know anything about Rels personally?" asked Rins. All faces turned eagerly toward Silvers.

"We? No."

A faint hum of disappointment from the multitude.

"Don't worry. Most of us don't. But should you meet them, get a photo or autograph, or learn anything at all, please share it with us. On to new news!"

"Sit down now," whispered Ayrds.

"Yeh, verily, okay."

Syns sank back into their seat. Silvers! Never in all their novels had a character been saddled with such a ridiculous name. But the fans welcomed Silvers. They understood. Tears welled behind their visor.

". . . we could see light in the tower until midnight." A shepherd with crook had joined Rins on the podium. "No sightings so far this morning."

"Thank you. Olden business?" No one spoke. "Okay then, Nys."

A fan in a leather jerkin took the stage.

"Hail Nys," said Rins.

"Hail Nys," yelled the group.

"Hail fans. We just got this photograph. You can see that it are definitely the Sovereign on the wall walk. There are more coming soon."

"Wonderful. Thank you."

More hailing.

The photograph was passed around. When their turn came, Syns' hands were as eager as the next. They recognized robe and crown but it was a fairly blurred photo in dim light. Still, it were Rels and their heart beat harder.

"Time for the song, then," said Rins.

A groom Syns recognized, Futs, shouted, "Wait!"

Hails.

"We have a Cyras report. They rode yesterday and were in a very bad mood."

Most of the room seemed cheered by this information. Syns felt their own heart lift. Hah!

"Verily if there is no other news it's time for the song."

A courtier took the stage, lute in hand.

"Hail Rums," said Rins.

Unenthusiastic hails from the group.

"Thank you everyone. This is a new song we finished yesterday. For those interested in learning it, we will have a song session this evening at the usual time. It's a happy tune called Heart of Our Hearts."

Rums began. They were a bad lutenist, had a tuneless voice, and wrote terrible lyrics.

Syns were seized with restlessness. "Thanks," they whispered to Ayrds, rising, trying not to clank.

Outside they glanced at the castle; the tower windows were dark, the battlements empty.

"Silvers! Wait!" Ayrds ran toward them. "Where are you going?"

"Errands to do."

"We were wondering, you're smaller than we are, and we are the smallest knight. Are you coming to the school?"

"Uh, no, actually."

"Your voice sounds rather old. No offense."

"Yeh."

"So that's just a costume. Very nice." They inspected it more closely.

Syns held their breath.

"Good job, whoever made it. It looks like real armor. But it isn't, is it?"

"As a matter of fact it is."

"Oh. Well, that's unusual. If you weren't so old you know, or so short . . . no offense."

"None taken. Verily. See you."

"Did you know there are five meetings every day? This one which is very big, ten a.m. is small, noon is fairly big, three p.m. is small, and seven p.m. is like this one, really big."

"You go to all of them?"

"We have to miss ten because of school. And we're usually late to three because of training, but otherwise, yeah. You should see all the photos we've collected from Sovereign Secrets. We'll show you a copy."

"Great. Hey thanks. See you."

"Yeah. See you."

They parted ways as others emerged and dispersed. No one paid attention to the fan in a knight's costume who stole to the back gate and went through.

Syns walked to camp, blank with spent emotion. They gave Whooshes a workout and grooming, then crawled into their tent and fell asleep.

Eleven fans sat in a tithe of chairs circled at the front of the room. Syns had awakened and come to the three o'clock meeting.

Rins were there. "Ah, Silvers, glad to have you with us again." Syns recognized no one else.

The group were introduced. The structure was generally the same but without the hails and everyone could talk whether they had news or not. At one point Ayrds in their surcoat and Winches, a young knight in full armor, joined the circle. Ayrds gave Silvers a friendly nod.

People were talking about dreams, thoughts, wishes. Syns said nothing. They were overwhelmed by the honesty, the lack of shame. Syns had never known such things existed. With effort they kept still while behind their visor their eyes watered and their nose ran.

At the end of the meeting everyone stood, held hands, and chanted, "Rels, Rels, Rels, Rels, *Rels! We love you!*"

Syns sobbed but no one noticed.

They were back in the forest. "Whooshes, old buddies. Don't know if we can manage the fan club. Going to rust out our armor." But an ache in their heart were eased. They slept well.

The next day they returned for the seven a.m. meeting. That day they attended them all.

Thus began the fan club phase of our hero's life. In many ways it was the happiest time since the turn; in fact, since as far back as they could recall.

Several days later Syns spoke. It was at the three o'clock meeting after a surreptitious offer of whiskey and a straw from Nyes. Fans were inordinately helpful and generous. Why? Presumably because of the depth of understanding among them. And to prove the sanity of the enterprise. And perhaps something else: in the face of such potential humiliation, the trust that was needed.

"We fell in love with Rels at the High Summer Tournament," said Syns. Many nods and sympathetic murmurs. "It have been painful, mostly. We feel so hopeless about it. But you all understand. Thank you."

They had done it. They had named their love. No one had laughed or guffawed or shown by the slightest twitch that they found this love absurd. The words were a watershed, the most honest ever spoken in their life.

Having done it once, Syns spoke at every meeting they could. The more they spoke the better they felt. They were not unique; they were like every other poor fool in love with Rels, dreaming and pining. It were almost adequate at times, being hopeless but so accepted.

Listening to the others, Syns came to know them individually. Everyone were different, loved Rels in a slightly different way. Syns felt compassion for all.

In their declarations some of the fans appeared not to suffer, a phenomenon Syns found astonishing. Perhaps the real knights had reason to hope, but the shorts, how did they arrive at equanimity?

Some members joked all the time. Syns knew they hurt the most. Our hero were amazed that there were people who were even more neurotic than themselves.

The fan club was a limitless purveyor of data about the Sovereign. In prior times when Syns had loved from afar, they had known almost nothing of the beloved. Now every microscopic event was noted and discussed.

There were theories and rumors about Rels' entire life. What was certain was that they had come to H-town only two months prior. The former Sovereign had re-signed suddenly a couple of weeks before that. Rels were crowned at the Midsummer Faire on July first, only four-teen days after their arrival. Everyone had to have a job.

After the coronation Cyras had gone to pay homage to the new Sovereign and had become their chosen knight. Whether or not they were lovers was uncertain, the source of endless speculation and disagreement. It was Syns' opinion that everyone fervently hoped they weren't, includ-ing those who said they didn't care and those who, even more improbably, professed to be in favor of the union.

Something between Rels and Cyras had happened at the High Summer Tournament. Whatever it was, it had caused the Sovereign to take to the tower accompanied by their immediate court and staff. They refused all visi-tors, including Cyras.

Alms, who came to meetings a few times a week, were an attendant to Rels. They were willing to talk about the Sovereign's moods and activities but consistently refused to provide photographs or anything too personal. They reported that overall Rels seemed rather weary but they were holding up. They were conducting business and al-ways gracious, even when not in the best of moods. Alms had served under the prior Sovereign who had not been well-liked. Rels were far more beloved by everyone at court.

Syns were comforted by Alms' reports. Rels were as good as they appeared to be. But the reports were also unsettling: Rels were human—they had to have some imperfections, didn't they?

This Beauty

Syns were walking back to the forest one evening after the seven p.m. meeting. The summer light was lingering. Looking up at the sky, an inhalation of hope and well-being. Tears. In love, seeing everything through this lens of tears.

This beauty explodes out of our eyes and lands on everything we see. The world could not be more enchanting. So alive, like a child's view, sparkling light and leaves, melody of wind.

We are undone. This unspeakable loveliness, the price and bonus of our love—that which it extract and that which it bestow beyond measure—robbing us of solidity and heaping upon us the bounty of radiance and rapture.

We are as a child again, inhabiting the realm of unblunted sensation, love, and striving.

Twisted

A love that have sacrificed everything into the furnace of necessity, twisting reality like heated glass so that the other may stand incontestably desirable.

In the process of love there comes a change, when the attachment to being in love are greater than the attachment to reality. And then? You must simply await disillusionment. This is the function of the devils, to bring us our necessary disenchantment, that we may open our eyes again from the blindness of our romance.

Meanwhile the task of twisting reality requires so much effort it makes us almost incapacitated.

The devils? They are but the envoys of time. Though we fear them they are our rescuers. Through them shall change come, to extricate us from our imaginary world, from our psychotic necessity.

Presence

When one are separated from the beloved, one must imagine that they are nigh. Syns felt the presence of Rels in the forest. They had conversations and arguments, a relationship with its ups and downs.

Master Plan

There were people in the Fan Club whom Syns would have liked to become friends with. Syns would have liked to reveal their identity to them, to reveal everything. But they could not because they had a master plan. Perhaps the others had master plans too.

Syns': to win the beloved in actuality.

A Crowded Life

Though life consisted only of going to meetings and going back to the forest and caring for Whooshes, Syns' days were crowded now.

The fan club was always doing something for Rels. Sending a card. Making a gift. Syns got involved in everything.

Teeth

Syns awakened from a dream of Rels' teeth. Looming like buildings, like a mountain range.

Undertow

Although life were lived in the presence of great beauty in the forest and great fellowship at the dance pavilion, there was a constant undertow, the unceasing wish to be with the beloved. Wondering what they were doing this minute, and this. Missing them, as if one had been with them and were parted. Wanting to be with them *again*.

Not Twin Souls

Irrespective of differences, love occur. As reports, photographs, and rumors came in, Syns realized that Rels and they were not twin souls after all.

What should we do? Tolerate the difference. We must remain ourselves, which cannot be changed anyway.

When Syns would learn of a difference they would not think of it as a problem; instead they would hold it as a question. For example, Rels had arrived in H-town on a motorcycle. Syns held it as a question: Why?

Insanity

After the initial relief and cure of the fan club, difficulties returned. Syns felt they were slowly going insane. They tried to imagine that someday their love would settle down and be in the past. Would they say, "What was *that*?" Would they have learned anything?

Many of the fans attributed cosmic meanings to their feelings. Our hero thought their own love were accidental, a fluke. A more disabling theory.

They felt so weary. Moody. Weak. And happy. And miserable.

The Fish Trap

You don't choose to swim into the fish trap but it happens. It is almost impossible to swim out. Mainly because meaning accumulates upon you like crystals in a supersaturated solution. You grow so big with meaning you cannot swim out again.

Not only that, meaning takes on a life of its own. It

becomes essential. Were you to stop being in love, meaning would vanish—it would go in one door of the cuckoo clock and absurdity would pop out the other.

The loss of ones' heavy coat of meaning becomes something to fear.

Information

Even with the fan club, so much Syns could not know.

Everyone wanted what was best for Rels but knew not what that was. They wanted desperately for Rels to be happy.

Syns were painfully aware that they did not know how they could be of any help to the Sovereign. They did, however, learn every muscle of the face in every expression, the wardrobe, the stances of the body.

As for Rels' thoughts, they became known from time to time. For example, Alms related that one evening Rels were talking about love. The club went rigid as hounds. Rels had said that love were overblown, that it were not as important as friendship. Syns were shocked to their toes. Then they held it as a question—why?—and recovered.

Innocence

The generosity and honesty of the fan club members never failed to touch Syns. There was a heartbreaking innocence to it, even regarding sexuality. In the small meetings people would sometimes relate their fantasies. They spoke, they listened to each other, unperturbed. About such things Syns never said a word.

Daily Life

Syns usually woke up with the thought that Rels were waking up also. An almost unbelievable fact, that Rels were a real person having a real life.

Daily tasks become magical acts when done by the beloved.

Floating

In a way Syns lost themselves, evaporated, because their consciousness were so focused on Rels. In a way they became a consciousness without an ego.

A sense of freedom and floating. A difficult state in which to get anything done.

Hostility

Some people in the fan club were hostile, yet they were regarded with compassion. Perhaps they served the group, manifesting the anger that others felt but could not express. With so much suffering it would have been surprising if hostility were not present.

117

Vulnerability

Being in love and being with others who were in love with the same person, Syns' old feelings of inferiority were frequently aroused. They had a reason why every other fan were more likely to win Rels than themselves.

It was clear that others had the same problem. Almost everyone felt inadequate at times.

Growth

It upset Syns that the fan club was growing. How dare anyone join after they did!

The Same Love

Sometimes you love something so private that only you know of it. Sometimes you love something so public that everyone know. The same love either way, the same surrender and force.

It are your own manner of love spilling out of your heart, as vision spills out of your eyes.

In the Offing

A moment in the summer evening when shadows race across the street to blind the backs of the leaves, to cover the near earth with darkening light.

Romance of Romance

A whisper of the coming autumn, the story that will be told in all sincerity, all perplexity—the portent of endings, the season of hymns.

Every Quality

One morning Alms reported that Rels had been irritable the night before. The fans were delighted. Every quality was endearing.

At first the beloved must fit the image of love. Later they define it.

No Gifts

Ayrds once complained to Syns that Rels never sent anything to the club. "In most fan clubs the members would get something special now and then, a gift or a visit."

To Syns the idea was unimaginable. They could not even tell if they would want such things.

One Subgroup

There were one subgroup that met late on some nights. The talk was of the most extreme sexual fantasies, graphically described. The membership were surprising; you would not have predicted that these mild-mannered fans harbored such thoughts.

Syns went once. They didn't go back.

Hard to Imagine

Our vision has configured Rels, especially their face, to our desire.

So hard to imagine that in the past others fell in love with us, that their eyes configured our own face to their desire. Some even suffered.

An Off-Putting Habit

We dreamed we were hired as Rels' bodyguard, to keep away all the unwanted fans and stalkers. We told Rels that they should develop an off-putting habit, like letting food dribble down their chin when they ate.

We awoke thinking it was a brilliant idea. We wouldn't mind. Everything about Rels was appealing.

Rins

The leader of the fan club were a short with a loud nasal voice. Syns were in awe of their forthrightness, their lack of shame, their firm belief that Rels were to be shared.

Obligation

If you love someone, perhaps you are obliged to pursue them so that they have the opportunity to love you in return.

Flaw

Syns worried that Rels had a tragic flaw. In the past their intuition was usually correct; the flaw they had imagined proved to be present and fatal for love.

What would it be with Rels? There would be no communion of souls—Rels would not want it or even be able to understand what it were.

If ever we were to get together with Rels and then we discovered that our intuition were correct, and we left them, Rels would be fine. All our ex-lovers did fine. It has never been the end of the world to be left by us.

Always Surprised

Syns could never imagine that their love could grow stronger. They were always surprised.

Smile

Rels had an incredible smile: exuberant, knowing, and compassionate. Syns would look at a photograph thinking, O to be smiled upon—surely better than sex.

Actions

By showing up at the fan club meetings you were active. Speaking and listening were actions.

Eating

Alms reported that when Rels thought no one were watching, they were a messy eater. Some fans were appalled. Syns were delighted because they did the same thing. It was a bond.

Photographs

When a new photograph would arrive it was like a feeding frenzy of piranhas. Sometimes photos would appear that had been taken before the turn. Rels with Cyras. It was always painful for Syns to see them. After awhile the images would fade in their mind, mercifully.

Difficult Things

Scheduling time in the day to cry.

Being quiet and paying attention.

Sometimes so exhausted, wanting to do nothing. No, that was wrong. Not wanting to do nothing either.

The forbidden thought: if we knew them we might not be interested. Why was it forbidden? Why could Rels reject us in all wisdom but if we were to reject them it would be unforgivable?

With new information there sometimes came shock, aridity, cramped finitude, where once there had been a liquid infinity of emotion.

Prayer

Syns wanted lasting love. They prayed, Let it work out this time. Then they thought, What a ridiculous prayer, that we be happy while others are miserable. So they prayed for an to end to the suffering of all. Another prayer that didn't last.

Envy

At times it seemed inevitable to Syns that Rels would fall in love with them. They worried that the other fans would be envious. They didn't want to hurt their feelings. Some fans felt the way Syns did and some didn't.

Which would be best for Rels, someone who didn't want to hurt anyone's feelings or someone who didn't care?

One's Place

Eventually Syns found their place in the group. They were always helpful. They had no ambition to rise in the leadership hierarchy, nor for any special consideration.

Syns' hiding of face and body caused the fan club to settle at a distance from them. They were not in the innermost circle despite coming to all the meetings and speaking.

Syns understood the distance, understood that their

concealment violated the unwritten code of revelation. It could not be helped.

In a way Syns fell in love with everyone in the fan club, everyone in the world. They loved everyone but wanted only Rels.

Rumor

Syns had been attending the fan club meetings and going back to the forest for eight days, though it seemed like a lifetime.

It was the seven p.m. meeting. Veps, a delivery cart driver, stood. After the hails they asked, "Have anyone heard the rumor that Rels are going to step down from being the Sovereign?"

It was as if everyone in the room had bumped into an electric fence. There was a gasp. All heads turned to Alms the insider.

"No," said Alms, "we haven't heard anything like that. But, hmm, it *has* seemed that there's been something on their mind. Where did you hear this, Veps?"

"Ah, we don't like to reveal our sources. Let's just say we have our informants."

Syns were overcome. Rels step down! Their world was shattered.

Rins were unable to keep order. Everyone began talking at once, standing and milling around. The meeting was adjourned but a large group remained, to which Syns gravitated, as did Rins and Nys. No one could stop talking. Some people who had left returned with blankets and pillows. They were going to stay as long as it took to find out what was going on.

Rins said there was an unused room to the side of the dance floor where they could stay. It was turned into a twenty-four hour news center and camping facility with a hand-painted sign above the door: Emergency Lounge.

"Excuse me," said Syns, "is there somewhere we could keep our horse?"

Rins said they could use a small outbuilding behind the pavilion.

Syns rushed to the forest, packed, jumped on Whooshes, and galloped into M. The horse might be recognized but Syns were too distraught to care.

When Whooshes were tended to and secured for the night, Syns went over to the lounge.

Fourteen people were there, some in work clothes, many dressed for bed. Syns took off their armor but the visored helmet stayed on. Gossip and chatter continued for hours. Syns were reminded of the muckers, the comfort of other human souls around them at night, this time joined in worry, love, and understanding. Finally they drifted off to sleep.

The lounge was casual, many fans stayed in their bedclothes all day long. Others dropped in at all hours for updates and to discuss how they were feeling.

Syns had never talked so much. They were not even sure what they were saying. They simply opened their mouth and set free whatever words had gathered there.

Love and worry. For so many in the fan club, Syns included, worry was the proof of love as well as its sustainer— worry about how the other were doing and about whether they would abandon or betray you. The pain of these thoughts was necessary for maintaining love. With luck you found lovers who obliged this need.

At times Syns almost wanted Rels to find another love if it would make them happy.

But now there was the rumor, this overwhelming worry. Why would Rels step down? Syns' imagination came up with many possibilities: they were dying, they were ill, they were depressed, they were sick of H-town, they hated the fans, they didn't feel appreciated enough, they were bored. All reality shrank down to the rumor and collapsed like a black hole. Was it true? What did it mean? What would happen to the fan club? What good were being a knight if Rels were no longer the Sovereign? Absurdity on absurdity, a house of cards teetering on a house of cards.

The longest free fall so far. Caring so much with no control. Their heart were broken yet still breaking. A stinging in the eyes and throat as if one were trapped in smoke. And in the chemical fire, love burned more brightly than before.

We are not strong. We have no sense of humor.

Syns lost all awareness of themselves as someone separate from Rels. Their entire consciousness were given over to helpless devotion. They were shriveled, cowering in tears and obsession. Had there been an opportunity for action they could not have moved.

In the lounge the cares and concerns that helped to balance daily life broke down. Jobs were abandoned, relationships, obligations, pleasures.

Syns felt trapped. If Rels were actually in trouble they could not abandon them now. They must wait to be the one abandoned.

They resumed drinking—like many—heavily. Drinking, praying, weeping, talking, all to lessen the pain of overweening empathy.

A new photograph arrived of Rels on the wall walk in full regal costume. Looking happy. On seeing the photo something died for Syns. They walked outside. It was early morning, the infernal dew was on the cursed thorn.

"You are smiling?" Syns muttered. "You think this is a joke? You do not care how much we love you, how much we suffer for you? We thought we knew you. Don't you know that it is a great crime to treat love cavalierly? You *owe* it to us to take our love seriously. You do not talk to us, do not tell us of your plans. And you dare to smile while we weep for you. In effect you say our feelings for you are so unimportant you will not bother to explain anything to us. We hate you."

All this love and adoration had changed the Sovereign. "We do not care any more. You are less now, we can no longer love you." Needless to say, tears were streaming. We know how to get over love, Syns thought. You take a break. Gradually the features of the other become indistinct, until they are no longer the organizing principle of your eyes. Heartache attenuate and one day it are no more. Devotion are done, the goose of love are cooked. And some time later you love another.

128

Then Syns began to blame themselves for falling in love in the first place, for their hasty bad judgment. But they were still angry at Rels and this was new. "Have you no heart? We do our best to love you, our very best to share you, to be generous. And you do *nothing*, you say *nothing*. Do you enjoy our suffering? Do you like this power you have over us? We cannot forgive you."

Nys came outside, fuming. "You saw the photo?"

"Yeh."

"We could spit nails."

"Yeh. Screw 'em. We don't trust them anymore."

"What ignorance."

Ignorance seemed mild. Were that it, were Rels unaware of how they felt? "You think they don't know?" asked Syns.

"You think they do?"

"How could they not? We send cards and gifts all the time. How could they not know how much we love them?"

"They could be completely mentally retarded."

"Yeh."

"We're still in love. Are you?"

"No. It're over," said Syns.

"Well, good luck. Got a meeting coming up."

"See you."

Nys went back in. Syns had the sensation of standing on the deck of a ship and looking back at the shore, watching the land grow smaller, more irrelevant, as they moved away into the open sea.

If we never love again we will be okay. It are not necessary. We have learned something: you never promised
us anything. We invented it. Now we feel betrayed. The
world creaks on its axis, burdened with its cargo of real
suffering, while we have an emergency lounge because
you *might* be unhappy. Fine. Now we hope you *are* unhappy. If you do not know you hurt us, that hurts us too.
And another thing, we are through crying for you. With
that thought they cried even harder.

Now what? Try not to get ill. Let time pass. Where
shall we go? Syns did not have the strength to go anywhere—not back to the forest or the muckers or the Butts
or the cottage. They went back to the lounge because it
was possible.

There were a group that played endless games of cards.
Syns joined them and played nonstop for two days. While
their attention was otherwise occupied, love crept back
in. But a cherished myth was destroyed, the myth that
Rels sensed that Syns were out there. They had held the
belief, despite their pragmatic way of thinking, that the
turn had created a mystical connection between them.
Was it not the case that the first time Syns looked at Rels,
the Sovereign had rejected Cyras?

Later that day Alms rushed in, breathless. "Only got
a moment. It're definite. They're not stepping down."

The Emergency Lounge lasted one more day while
everyone talked and recovered.

Then Syns, exhausted, rode back to the forest.

Broken

BACK AT CAMP some leaves and needles had fallen and there were several new spider webs. Otherwise it was as they had left it.

Syns felt broken, humbled yet another level. Understanding that to be human was to be close to madness at all times. Knowing that their quest was futile. All they wanted to do was to serve. In a way, feeling purified. Yet wondering how long they could endure this life.

They no longer had the slightest hope that love could nourish or sustain them. They were physically much weaker. There was no foreseeable happiness. Their old life was gone; now the goal was survival without illusions, using will and brute force.

Rels' worthiness no longer mattered. If they won them they would remain with them, broken hero that they were.

Cold

AFTER SETTING UP CAMP AND TENDING to Whooshes they turned in.

With a tickling throat they awoke in the night, with a runny nose in the morn. They had an excuse to do nothing except keep warm, rest, drink hot fluids.

And do something about boredom. What did knights in the forest do when they caught a cold? Sharpen their swords and write poetry, most likely, but it was too much trouble.

They had a couple of books Rums had given them. Syns found one, a romance novel by an author far less successful than themselves.

They made a hot toddy and snuggled down.

The plot was predictable, the characters thin, the language stilted, the emotions wooden, the facts wrong, the sex scenes—simply had to be skipped over. But it made you weep and it had a happy ending.

It was comforting.

After finishing the book they slept a long time. They awoke feeling feverish. Their ears rang. Trying to stand they trembled, fragile as a soap bubble.

The day was overcast and cool, the best weather for burrowing down in your tent, snoozing, drinking another hot toddy.

In love we reencounter the world, changed. We had never been interested in romance novels and, despite our career, had prided ourselves on the fact that we had never read one. Now we had, and even enjoyed it. One more proof of the softening of our brains.

Nostalgia

THEY FELT SAFE IN THE WORLD, relaxed, when they awoke in the early evening. They stared up at the green canvas of the tent while recollections from childhood gathered together and dispersed.

The rock collection they had loved so passionately: dark flaking mica, red garnets embedded in granite, fools' gold, obsidian.

Other things that sparkled: glitter, tinfoil they crinkled into little animals, colored glass.

Things that shone: lightning bugs, candles, yellowed light through windows in winter.

Once, at a beach, they had found an abalone shell. A miraculous interior of silvery pink and turquoise.

Evening in a park. A small lake reflecting the setting sun. A circling white colonnade in the center.

A neighborhood of small pastel houses like valentine candies.

A covered cut-glass dish at some old relatives' apartment, filled with ribbon candy so big it was hard to fit in your mouth.

They fell asleep again.

Bittersweet

HACKING AND COUGHING the next morning. Wanting to read another romance. They found the other book, by an author even less auspicious than the first.

Cool gray-blue fog outside the tent. Shivering, they took care of Whooshes, then crawled back into their sleeping bag and sank into the book. It was dark when they finished it by lanternlight.

It had a sad ending. How dare they! Syns despised the bittersweet. What was the *point*?

Sign

THE BOOK MADE SYNS FEEL disconnected. Alone. Useless. Were they going to further their quest lying around escaping into bad romance novels?

Fear returned, and despair. The distraught knight called out, *"Show us a sign!"*

A bloodfreezing wail shattered the night.

Komodos

THE KOMODOS WERE AN INTERTWINING PAIR of roller-coasters in F. Despite the fact that they tended to fling passengers from side to side, a bruising and unpleasant experience, they were one of H-town's most popular attractions. There had been talk for years of upgrading to a newer, smoother, more terrifying model but nothing had ever come of it. Once a week they were lubed and tested. All of H-town were subjected to the horrible noises of the process.

Syns sprang from their sleeping bag, head a-fuzz but light on their feet. They barded their steed, threw on their armor, grabbed lance and sword, and galloped off.

For safety in the foggy darkness they chose a familiar route via the back gate of M and over the M-town–F-town bridge. There were a few nocturnal strollers in M but F was deserted. Even the zoo animals were bunked down for the night, probably covering their ears as best they could.

An attendant were beside the Komodos' electrical box when Syns galloped up.

Falling forward into action. So unlike us. "Stand aside!" shouted Syns, jabbing the air with their sword.

"Holy shits! Get back over to M where you belong, you crazy parentsfucker!"

"Stand back or we'll run you through."

Still cursing, the attendant scuttled off. Syns charged

at the electrical box. Sparks zapped far out into the air and along the blade as wires were attacked, knobs and switches went flying. There was an acrid chemical smell.

The Komodos screeched no more.

Syns raced over to the first dragon and wielded their sword against the red lizard-patterned naugahyde seats. They slashed them to ribbons. They rode to the second dragon and did they same with blue naugahyde.

The attendant were creeping back, keeping a good distance, muttering ". . . fucks fucks fucks fucks fucks . . ." Steady as a metronome.

Syns dismounted, grabbed wires and knobs, and wrapped them in swaths of red and blue, shouting, "Give this to Rels, Sovereign of M-town, with our humble compliments." They jumped on Whooshes and thundered off into the night.

Back at camp Syns were exhilarated. They waited for a response. Nothing happened. It occurred to them that no one knew where they were. But that should not stop love if love it doth inspire. We have done our part.

They felt in the peak of health. Cure for the common cold: sociopathy.

As usual there was too much time to think. The occasion of their first knightly deed deserved something special: they made coffee over the campfire and added a splash of whiskey.

At least we did something. If you encounter dragons, surely it is a sign you are on the right path.

Ah foolishness, the easiest way for one human being to become known to another. What if we had come upon real monsters, would we have been so brave?

Syns tried to stay awake, listening for sounds of alarum. It was the quietest night in a long time.

First Roust

IN THE MORNING STILL NOTHING.

As the day ground on, Syns became more frustrated. Surely the word was out. Surely the fan club had heard. Where the hells *were* everyone?

O irony—that the Sovereign in the tower have freedom and power whilst we, a poor knight in the forest, are in bondage to anxiety and fealty.

Perhaps the Komodos were not enough. Perhaps another deed was in order. What shall we fight next? And, more importantly, how can we be sure to be noticed?

Barded and harnessed, horse and rider arrived at the back gate of Old N. Syns lifted the latch and went through.

If walking in Old Normal in dirty serf-wear attracted attention, it were nothing compared to galloping through its streets in full armor. Passersby shouted, "Go back to your castle!" And worse.

Our hero, undeterred, headed straight for the thrift store at the opposite end of town. A banner proclaimed that it was senior discount day. Through the swinging glass door rode Syns. Shoppers hobbled out of their path.

They had never been inside before but a large part of their childhood had been spent with their parents in just such temples of the bargain.

The familiar poignant smell of objects being forgotten: old perfumes, dusts, molds. Dim lights, faint music, the mournful sound of scraping hangers.

A tarnished trumpet was on a top shelf behind the checkout counter, reserved for objects of greater value. Whooshes squeezed through the opening next to the counter while a checker shouted frantically into a telephone. The Silver Knight stood in the stirrups, grabbed the trumpet, and rode off.

Moments later, a siren. Citizens stopped on sidewalks to gape and point. A police car was gaining on the criminal. But hah! It was too big to get through the back gate. The officers jumped out and pursued on foot. The forest rang with whistles and shouts of "Stop, thief!" They were no match for Whooshes.

Back at camp the sounds of pursuit faded away. Syns removed price stickers and began polishing. It had been quiet for awhile so they raised the instrument to their lips. An ancient sweet smell of dried spit, oil, and brass. They managed to get out a few weak notes.

When evening came, horse and knight set out in gleaming armor with shining trumpet. Syns were fearful. They welcomed the feeling: it was the herald of adventure.

They dashed straight for the castle. As usual, admirers, primarily knights, lolled at the edge of the mote nearest the tower. There were about twenty of them, some with lutes or guitars, sending lovesick songs and poetry upwards.

When fifteen yards away, Syns gave a mighty trumpet blast, couched their lance, and galloped straight for the knot of swains. They scattered like feathers in the wind.

Syns were alone beneath the tower, heart pounding, hands shaking with anxiety and success. A better knight would have known what to do next. Their mind swirled like an emptying drain. After trotting around a bit they made a single bleat on the trumpet and rode back to camp.

They waited for summons, gratitude, challenge, combat. They remained in the saddle fighting fear and the inexorable march of self-doubt. Why was it that their deeds provoked no response? What made their inadequacy so evident?

A bat flew out from a decaying tree.

Second Roust

HUNCHED OVER IN THE SADDLE our knight awoke. Whooshes continued to sleep beneath them.

They dismounted and crept off to the tent. Later they awakened to another day in the indifferent, silent forest. There was only one course of action: keep on doing deeds until Rels took notice. Thus the knightly life.

To point a lance and charge a group of unsuspecting loiterers does not require great courage. But what if we were to return? The wooers were knights, likely be armed and ready to fight.

It was evening. Syns approached the castle. Almost all the knights in the kingdom were there—from Cyras, unbelievably tall on their gargantuan horse Phantoms, to several trainees who likewise managed to appear large and menacing. All were in full armor.

A crowd of eager-looking citizens had gathered.

A thought eased Syns' terror: most likely we aren't going to be killed. Or even maimed.

The trumpet call left something to be desired but the racing forward with readied lance was in admirable form.

The legion rode forward to meet them, lances poised. Just when it appeared that Syns were going to be dashed to the ground, or worse, the first knights parted and joined on the other side. They formed a wheel with twenty lances for spokes and Syns at the hub. They were laughing.

Someone in the crowd shouted, "Leave the youth alone."

"What think ye aren doing, knave?" roared Cyras.

The knights yea'd and snickered.

"We are a knight, come to defend the peace of the crown." Syns' voice, though cracking, was entirely audible.

"Ye aren naught but a fool. If ye persisten, ye will regretten it. Be ye warned, fool."

"We are not afraid of you. Let one of you step forward to fight in fairness." Syns prayed that no one would take up the offer.

"Ye aren no knight, but a foolish actor, unworthy of our time or skill. Nay, ye aren a rat, which deserven no fair fight, but only to be dispatched without pity."

"Oh yeah?"

"Ho ho! Ye aren unable even to speak improperly. Cometh knights, let us shew this low fool how we dispatch a rat!"

This was ridiculous. A double negative.

The wheel enlarged as the knights backed off. A moment later it shrank again as the spokes closed in on the hub.

The notes of a hunting horn poured over the land like honeyed nectar.

The knights stopped.

A commanding voice spoke: "Knights, disperse."

All eyes looked at Cyras. The giant looked at the tower, then back at Syns. "We aren not finished with yow," they sneered.

The gang cantered off with many a menacing look

back at our hero. Syns did not know if the edict included themselves or not. They waited. The crowd was quiet.

"Stranger, approach," said the voice.

Syns urged Whooshes over toward the tower, their chest tingling with amazement. Surely this was happening to someone else. Ah yes, to the brave knight they were impersonating.

The crowd sighed. One or two people clapped.

Castle

CRANING THEIR NECK, SYNS LOOKED UP at the tower's lone small window. Perhaps they saw a shape within, perhaps not.

There was the sound of approaching footsteps. A throat cleared. Syns looked over.

A liveried attendant said, "The Sovereign Rels command your presence in the tower."

Syns nodded, unable to speak. It was like a dream. The attendant held Whooshes' bridle as they moved toward the castle. The drawbridge had been lowered, the portcullis raised.

Another attendant appeared, saying, "We shall take good care of your steed. Fear not."

Still unable to speak, Syns dismounted.

"Pray, follow us," said the first attendant. Syns followed them across the bailey to the hall.

They had been here many times as a child, helping to build the castle in the limited but thrilling ways allowed to the children. Now everything shimmered in unreality.

They passed through the arched front doors and were in a screen passage. They went up a staircase on the left. They emerged into another hallway where sconces burned in the dimness. To their left a wall bowed into the room. In the wall's middle was a door. The attendant unlocked it with a large key. A curving staircase began at their feet. They were in the tower.

As they climbed, Syns looked closely at the stone wall. They reached over and touched it; the surface held an ancient coolness. For these moments, until their deceit was found out, they tried to absorb the reality of the situation. They wanted to remember forever this proximity to the beloved. They had an overpowering sense of good fortune, so intense they were almost numb.

The staircase ended at a heavy door. The attendant rapped and the door was opened from within.

Syns entered a circular room of unexpected spaciousness, hung with tapestries of purple, red, and gold. Clean rushes covered the floor, the scent of lavender wafted up. A low fire glowed in a great hearth.

There were around fifteen people in the room, some attending, some sipping from goblets and eating at small tables. Conversations stopped as everyone looked at the stranger.

Syns prostrated themselves upon the floor.

"Rise."

They lifted their head a few degrees. Someone were standing in front of them. They raised their head a few more degrees. A hand was reaching out toward them. They were too shaken to remember what they were supposed to do. They gave the extended hand a little squeeze. Their head remained mostly bowed, their eyes downcast.

"What are ye called?"

What are we called? A moment of breathtaking inspiration: "We are called the Silver Dwarf. We are but an unworthy knight and your most humble servant."

"Rise, Silver Dwarf Knight." The voice sounded faintly amused. "Perhaps ye would like to join us in dinner and wine."

"Yea, verily, your . . . sovereignness."

"Take off your helmet, then, and have a seat at the table with us."

The helmet! They could not risk it. "By your leave we prefer to keep it on."

"Well then, at least raise up your visor."

"By your leave we prefer to keep it lowered."

"Then how shall ye eat or drink?" The voice was definitely amused.

"Have you, a, uh, straw?"

"Verily, one shall be procured. Now come, follow us. We are not so formal here in the tower. We would be pleased to converse with you."

"Yes, your . . . grace." Syns rose but were still unable to lift their eyes.

After introductions to everyone, the Sovereign took the knight by the hand and led them to a table well away from the fire. Beside it were a carven throne and a chair. A goblet with a straw was soon delivered, as well as a bowl with what looked like thick soup and another straw.

Syns were suddenly starving and dehydrated. They took a sip from the goblet, slurping just a little. It were difficult to remember how to swallow.

"Tell us where ye are from, Silver Dwarf Knight."

"We are from . . . excuse us your highness." Syns gulped at the wine. How was it possible they were so unprepared? "We are from a small country. Far away. With a rich tradition of knighthood."

"Ah. And tell us, what is it that brings you here to Old Medieval-town?"

"Well, as you seem to have observed, tonight we tried to disperse the . . . other knights. We are deeply grateful to you for rescuing us. Your worship."

"As are we to you. The music and poetry disturbs our peace. And were it ye who dispatched the knights the evening before?"

"Yes your most nobleness."

"And the dragons? The hides and brains that were delivered to us? Ye did that also?"

"Yes your greatness."

"We are well pleased with you. Because of your devotion our nights have been much quieter."

"We are gratified that you find our humble attentions to your liking, your delightfulness."

"And have ye further ambitions, besides creating silence for our repose?"

Repose! Best not to think about that too much. What to say? Everything hinged on this moment. We wanted everything, therefore honesty was out of the question. We write—wrote—romances for a living, we could do this. "We are recently come to H-town and are awaiting assignment. We hope to be admitted to the privileged order of knights."

"Oh. Perhaps ye did not know. Only talls may be admitted."

"We know, your excellency. But we *are* a tall, in a manner of speaking."

"Certainly your speech is most tall."

"We mean, we are the child of talls, as far back as history goes. But we are unfortunately a dwarf."

"But ye are quite tall for a dwarf."

"Exactly. Because of the tallness of our people, even a dwarf are tall, for a dwarf."

"Ah. And what are your plans now?"

"To return to the forest and continue our quest to serve you, your worthiness."

"Ye live in the forest?"

"It is the proper place for a knight, your greatness."

"What is it like there? Is it comfortable?"

"In truth it is difficult at times. But we do not mind. Your superiorness."

"Hmm. In recompense for your bravery and the attentions ye have bestowed upon us, would ye like to spend a few days at the castle?"

Syns almost dropped the goblet. "We would be deeply honored, your . . . honor."

"Are ye weary from your labors? For, if so, ye may be shown to your chamber immediately."

Syns were so exhausted they could hardly keep their eyes open. But who knew how long this good fortune would last. They had to lift their eyes and look at Rels, it might be their only chance. After another slurp of wine, they did.

There were the Sovereign in crown and robe, every bit as stupefyingly wondrous as in the photographs. No, more so. It hit Syns like a fist to the solar plexus. "We . . . we . . . yes, we are very tired. We would like to rest, your . . . your wondrousness. But first we must attend to our horse."

"Your steed will receive the best of care here, should ye wish to leave them with our grooms. Goodnight then, Silver Dwarf Knight. Rest well and we shall see you on the morrow."

The hand was extended again. Syns managed to take it and look at it for a moment before curling further forward, practically in a swoon.

"We shall see to our horse ourselves. Goodnight, your stunningness."

Syns were escorted out the way they had come in, then across the bailey to the stables where Whooshes nuzzled them happily.

Later, Syns were led back to the hall, up the first stairs as before, and to the right to a bedchamber with its own small blaze in the hearth.

"Silver Dwarf Knight, a bath is prepared and clean bedclothes await you. Your armor and any effects ye wish shall be cleaned and attended to. Desire ye anything further?"

"No thank you."

When the attendant had gone Syns locked the door. They stripped down and sank into steaming water, fragrant with herbs. Heavens. They bathed and dried off with thick towels. They opened the door to the hall a fraction. The coast was clear. They set out everything for cleaning. Finally they crawled between silken sheets and slept.

Someone were knocking. Syns opened an eye, then two. It was day and it was not a dream. They were in the castle and Rels were pleased with them.

Is this, then, the deserved fruit of valor? Could it be that we are brave and loveable after all? No one else have been invited into the tower. Hah! One thing is clear: last night there were no one in the immediate vicinity who resembled a rival. Perhaps we shall do nothing but lie here for a few days and savor our triumph.

The knock repeated.

"Who are there?"

"Your attendant, Glurs. The Sovereign Rels have commanded you to dine with them."

Commanded! Our knight's heart leapt. They arose and opened the door a crack. "Hand us our helmet."

When helmet and visor were in place they admitted Glurs, bearing clean armor and garments.

Syns entered the tower chamber. Rels were alone, wolfing down a sandwich. Across from them were three large goblets with straws.

Rels nodded, Syns bowed, and Glurs withdrew.

"Good day, Silver Dwarf Knight. One goblet contains

orange juice, one coffee, the third a protein drink. We couldn't wait any longer."

"Good morning your brightness."

"Technically it's no longer morning. It's two in the afternoon. We have a surprise for you."

" Two? You do?"

"There are someone who wishes to meet you."

This could only be bad news. "Us? How is that possible? No one even know we are here."

"Your entry into the castle was observed by many. Furthermore, word travels fast concerning everything that transpires here. You would be surprised."

A thought brushed by like an unwelcome moth, of the fan club and its avidity for every molecule of information. "Really? That is too bad."

"You feel that way?"

"We do."

"Interesting. We hope you enjoy the surprise." There is a door behind us. Pray open it."

Afternoon of a Fan

SYNS OPENED THE DOOR AND GASPED. It were none other than the obsessed fan of Syns the writer. What to do, what to do. "We . . . we . . . have to see to our hor—"

"Worry not—"

"Silver Dwarf!" cried the fan.

Gads. The dwarf bit had come into existence only the night before.

The fan rushed up to Syns and grabbed their hand. "You don't know us yet, our name are Blats. We are your biggest fan! We love you so much! Can we have your autograph?" They held out a piece of red naugahyde and a marking pen.

Syns stared at the pen and hyde. What if their handwriting was recognizable? "Well, you know, we mean—"

"Please! We want to be the first! We used to be a fan of someone else, some writer. Much shorter, much less attractive. Not nice either. But who care, now we have you! So mysterious and brave and sexy—oops, sorry. Guess what? You already have a fan club! We started it last night. Only nine people so far, but give us time."

"Uh, well—" Syns didn't know whether to be flattered, insulted, or merely terrified.

Rels were grinning. "Silver Dwarf Knight. Give your fan your autograph."

Blats beamed. "Say 'To Blats with all our love from the Silver Dwarf.'"

Were Rels *winking* at us? "Alright, here you go."

"What about 'with all our love'?"

"Um. We only just met."

"That can be remedied," said Rels. Surely they weren't laughing. They turned toward Blats. "The Silver Dwarf Knight will be staying here at the castle for a few days. Ye are welcome to visit."

"Oh, *can* we?" Blats whispered. They flung themselves to the ground in a bow. "Thank you, thank you."

"In fact, would ye like to stay here too?"

"Here in the castle?"

"Verily. Our new knight need to get used to being admired."

"Oh! We admire them so much! We would love to stay in the castle!"

"The Silver Dwarf Knight are quite shy. We will send them to see you later. Meanwhile, if ye wait by the main door ye will be met and shown to a guest chamber." Rels rang the royal bell. An attendant entered and took the fan away.

Syns exhaled.

"You are troubled," said Rels

"Yes we are! We are a private person."

"You haven't been acting that way lately."

"That was to be noticed."

"And now you have been!"

"But not by fans!" Syns voice cracked with emotion. "We wanted to be noticed by . . . by . . . " They couldn't go on. They took a long sip of protein drink instead.

"It are refreshing to meet someone so modest. Most of the knights here thrive on attention. You must understand something: fans cannot help themselves. It aren't anything serious. They go through a phase of adoration. Fortunately it do not last."

The words stung our knight like wasps. Not serious? Being a fan were as serious as life and death. As sanity and insanity. "Well . . ."

"You amuse us. Your diffidence are quite disarming."

"O yeah, charming." Syns could not keep a note of bitterness from their voice. Yet even in their bitterness they were surprised that Rels would use the word diffidence. They felt a twinge of guilt for being surprised.

"You will need to get more at ease with the fans, and more courteous. Think of the task as part of chivalry."

"It's just that—"

"Don't worry. All will be well. We have meetings now. Shall we see you this evening for dinner?"

The Silver Dwarf stood and bowed low. "It shall be our pleasure, your commandingness."

Rels rang the bell. The main door opened and the court entered. Someone took Syns' chair while they and their drinks were moved across the room. They could not make out Rels' words but the Sovereign looked more serious, which were either a good sign or a bad one.

When Syns had finished their repast, Glurs appeared at their side. "What wish ye, Silver Dwarf Knight?"

To stay the hells away from the fan. "We would like to see our horse."

"There is a small riding courtyard here at the castle. We also have equipment for jousting practice, should ye desire it. Or if ye prefer, there is a larger field close by which is used by all the knights. We would make sure ye met with no harm."

"We would prefer to practice jousting here at the castle." By far.

When Syns arrived at the stables, a groom were in the process of barding Whooshes. Syns completed the task.

The courtyard was delightful. Earlier a light drizzle had dampened the earth and scents wafted over from the castle herb garden. It were a comfort to be on Whooshes, driving at the quintain and pretending it were Blats. When practice was over, Syns groomed their steed, who nuzzled them with affection.

Glurs showed up. "Would ye like to bathe?" It seemed to be the chief activity around here. What the hells. Might as well get as groomed as the horses.

Syns were back in their chamber, about to step into the bath, when there was a loud knock. "Glurs, are that you?"

"It are Blats."

Gads. "Oh."

"Have we offended you? You must know, there are nothing we wouldn't do for you. Nothing at all."

"Well, hmm. We could use a bit of privacy."

"For you and us?"

"No, actually we were just about to get into the bath."

A pause. "Ba . . . th?" The fan sounded as if they were having an asthma attack.

"Uh. Yes."

"We could . . . we could, um . . . scrub your back. Or get you something. Some chilled champagne. Candles."

"Actually, we'd like to bathe in a bit of . . . peace."

"You mean alone?"

"Exactly."

"How can you treat us like this?" Sniffling.

Syns felt bad. "Listen, we'll, see you later, okay?"

"You promise?"

Syns promised and footsteps shuffled off.

Syns sighed deeply as they sank into the bath. Nothing like this luxury at the muckers. Whatever happened to equality? It's not like the place was teeming with visitors wanting to peer at royalty. Rels carried on like this every day, as if they really *were* royalty. While some poor goatherds were out there, and psychiatric technicians, and bakers with their arms in hot ovens. Rels weren't who we thought they were. They lacked empathy, lacked perception. They were far too comfortable with privilege. Syns slid lower into the tub and out of love altogether.

Soaked and dried they suited up in their armor. Since we are no longer in love, it's time to go.

They toppled onto the bed in misery. They pulled the silks over their eyes, vanquished by the absence in their heart where once had dwelt their love.

This Potempkin village of love. Contemptkin village are more like it. Blats think they love us and therefore we owe them something. Their idea of love is a license to demand our attention, to *demand* our love in return. And then they are weeping because we want to be left alone. As if we had injured them. We never asked for this. Time to get back to the forest. But it took so long to get here. Why are we so upset anyway? So some poor deluded soul think they are in love with us. Haven't we wept? Haven't we been just as nuts? They make us dislike and doubt ourselves. They make us feel so damned guilty. Who can be in love when they feel guilty? We can't. Guilt are the antidote to love.

After awhile Syns' despair died down. They were almost comatose. Then, in the ashes of burnt love, something ignited: anger. Not knowing what else to do, they lay there and felt its heat. For once in their life, anger incinerated guilt. We hate Blats. Maybe it are wrong but we hate them.

Anger kindled something else which lit up with a tentative flame: desire for Rels.

They peered into the hall and saw Glura, alone and snoozing. "Psst."

"Good day, our liege."

"Could you tell Rels we want to see them?"

"They are expecting you."

"Yes, but without the fan. We do not want to see the fan at all."

The attendant left and returned. "The matter are resolved."

Entering the tower chamber, Syns found Rels alone, stacks of paperwork on the table in front of them.

"There are something you would like to discuss?" asked the Sovereign. They set down their quill while Syns forgot to bow.

"Yes. It is about the fan. We know you find it amusing, but the fan knocked on our door awhile ago and started weeping when we wouldn't let them come in. We were about to get into the bath."

Rels started to smile.

"Don't smile. We are different from you. We do not find it amusing. We hate it to the depths of our being."

"Why?"

"The fan make us feel helpless and evil."

"If you are to be a complete knight, you must understand the fans. We cannot always choose who want to be close to us."

"How do *you* cope?"

"We recognize it as part of our job. There is a price to pay for being the Sovereign."

"What do you do if they weep?"

"It are difficult, even frightening at times. People beg, threaten to hurt themselves or us. You see this pile of letters?" Rels pointed to the tallest stack. "Fan mail. We answer it as best we can. Ultimately it are for the success of M, of H-town as a whole. When you have been here longer you will understand that everyone here work hard. Usually without complaint."

Syns knew they were being advised and chastened. "Don't you ever get fed up with it?"

"It are demanding. We do not do as much as are asked of us. But we do what we can."

"And what of your privilege? Not everyone in H-town have attendants at their beck and call."

"But how many people request—"

A messenger burst in. "Sorry to interrupt, your excellency. But the delegation from—"

"Oh, yes. We are most sorry Silver Dwarf Knight, but these visitors have traveled a long way. As for dinner, we apologize. It might be best if ye ate with the court in the great hall."

Syns nodded and left. So much for being special.

They spent the rest of the day with Whooshes. They felt so restored they decided to brave another encounter with the fan.

They met in a small reception chamber on the first floor. They both apologized. A few moments later the fan were weeping and threatening to harm themselves; the Silver Dwarf were shouting for help.

Attendants appeared instantly.

Syns were yelling, "We do not love you and we never will!"

Another Surprise

OUR KNIGHT HAD NO DESIRE to dine with the court. They preferred the company of Whooshes and the stable hands, which brought back fond memories of the muckers. Later they bathed and went to bed.

Rels were still busy with the delegation the next day. Syns went off to the stables. They were beginning to miss the Sovereign.

The following morning our knight were donning their armor for another session of jousting practice when Glurs knocked. "The Sovereign command a meeting as soon as ye are able."

"Do you know what it're about?"

"Only that it are to be a private meeting."

Syns' heart quickened. Perhaps—no, it couldn't be.

They were alone in the tower with Rels.

"Come, Silver Dwarf Knight. Sit with us." Rels were looking at them in a kindly fashion. "We don't know if you are familiar with the custom of sponsorship."

Ye gods it *were* happening.

Rels continued, "The sponsor give a token to their knight at the festivals. Though the relationship are chaste, ideally anyway, courtship are nonetheless involved: private meetings, exchanges of letters, attendance at sundry social occasions. The knight become the champion of their sponsor. Do you understand?"

Behind Syns' visor, tears were springing to their eyes.

They had to speak. "Oh Sovereign, a champion are what we most fervently wish to be."

"Excellent. We had hoped you would feel this way. Since you are a dwarf, your tallness are not visible, and some will disapprove, the other knights especially. But most of us are more open-minded. Deliberation have been given to the matter and a decision arrived at. We find you in all respects—save stature and your problem with fans—to be in possession of the fundamental qualities of knighthood: bravery, thoughtfulness, respect and sincerity. We find you to be worthy."

Worthy. A sweeter word was never heard in this lifetime. If the knights don't like it, hah!

"We have discussed the matter with others. They are of a similar opinion."

"That are excellent news."

"We wished to discover your feelings on the matter in private, before sending forth a public announcement. You would be surprised at how news and baseless rumors travel out from here. These things are capable of causing suffering."

Suffering? Were Rels saying that they would feel bad if we turned them down? "How can you imagine that our reply could cause suffering? We wish only to serve, and most humbly." Syns' heart were pounding and their breath was shallow.

"Such certainty are what we had hoped for."

"Your perfectness, this are the greatest honor of our

life. We mean it." Syns were suffused with joy so intense it bore no connection whatsoever to reality.

Rels rang their bell and the entire court filed in. "We are delighted to announce that the Silver Dwarf Knight have enthusiastically accepted."

"Yea," rasped Syns, "we are excited and thrilled to be a champion, and for the finest, most illustrious, most captivating person we have ever beheld." Syns fell to their knees and pressed their visor to the floor.

"Rise, Silver Dwarf Knight. We are verily pleased with you."

Syns stood and raised their head. A silken square of bright blue cloth was extended toward them.

Syns looked up into the expectant face, then over at Rels, who were beaming. "Take the favor, Silver Dwarf Knight, of our good cousin Tels, your sponsor."

Syns stared in utter, utter . . . there were no words. Their fingers somehow closed around the fabric. They knew they were supposed to treat it like a cherished object but it was all they could do not to drop the thing on the floor and stomp on it.

Rels approached. "Let us be the first to kiss you, in our pleasure at this union. May Tels and ye be ever happy, sponsor and champion." The Sovereign bent slightly and kissed our knight on their visored lips. A cheer went up from the court.

It were the most unhappy kiss of Syns' life. They turned, clattered down the stairs, rushed down the next set of stairs, flew outside, and dashed across the bailey to the stables. Whooshes were barded for jousting. Our hero jumped on and bounded across the lowered drawbridge.

Pitching Forward

BACK AT CAMP IN ARCADY. Their heart were broken for good. Were ever a knight more forlorn? Surely the greatest proof that you are unloved are that the other give you to yet another.

To Tels. There were nothing wrong with them except that they were *not Rels*. And, coward that we were, when we realized the disastrous error, we still took the favor, we committed. We are trapped.

Rels would never never know. Even if they did they would not care. O, they would be gracious about it, they had made that clear. Gracious and kind, as they were to all the poor slobs in love with them.

And worst of all, the kiss. On the lips, technically. How they had dreamed of it. Thank gods for the visor. For if . . . lips had met lips . . . it were unthinkable. They would have done something. Who know what, but it would have been disgraceful. Probably nothing, the most disgraceful act of all.

After a forest gallop and horse grooming, Syns set off on foot into the deeper woods. They knew not where they walked, blinded by confusion and misery.

They stumbled on the root of a tree and pitched forward.

Book Three: A Door in the Forest

While We Have Breath

THEY WERE FLAT ON THE GROUND with the wind knocked out of them. They lay awhile. When they picked themselves up they gasped.

The offending root extended from a tree in whose trunk was a door, slightly open. Syns knocked, then shouted.

Silence.

Are we a knight or aren't we? For lack of anything better, let us proceed as if we are. They slid their fingers behind the door and pulled. It creaked forward on stiff leather hinges.

"Hulloo? Anyone here?"

They entered. The scent of old smoke and a much more pungent smell of mold. The only light wandered in through the door. They saw a table holding three dust-covered objects: a candle, a metal match container, and something they did not recognize. They took out a match and lit the candle.

The walls of the small room were covered in markings. They picked up the candle and held it near a wall:

> That Love are all there are
> Are all we know of love
>
> For love ar'n of sae mickle might
> That it all paines maken light

Comfort us with love
For we are sick of apples

Love bear both the gonfanon
And banner of fair courtesy
It are wellmannered, sweet,
Frank and gentle, so that
Whoever may decide
To serve and honor it
No villainy nor treason
Nor any evil thought may dwell with them

Sniff the sweet omao scents of the grasses
The sweet scents of the wild vines
That are twisted by the winds
Ae our flowers
As if motes were in our eyes
Our makapo pupils are troubled
Dimness covers us
Woe are we

Hundreds of poems and quotations in neat columns.
Who had done this? Why? What had become of them?
The candle guttered and went out. They turned back to
the table and relit it. They spied the third object and wiped
off the moldy dust.

A bell jar.

They lifted the glass top with care. Revealed was an

embroidered velvet pouch. They carefully loosened the drawstring top and reached their fingers inside. They withdrew several scraps of beautiful paper. Something was written on each scrap in fine calligraphy:

That we should love bright particular stars
And think to wed them, they are so far above us

All lovers are warriors
And Cupids have their camps

These mentions of love throughout history were oil upon the troubled waters of their soul. They were not the first to love and to suffer, they would not be the last.

They took the pouch and went outside. When they pushed the door closed it groaned shut, clicked, and disappeared into the trunk.

For the next several days Syns worked around camp until the afternoon, then went on long rambling walks, sometimes not returning until late at night. They read and reread the scraps. In the dark they recited them from memory:

Romance of sorrow
Which transform sadness into beauty

Love suffereth long, and are kind
Love envieth not

Love vaunteth not itselves
Are not puffed up
Love beareth all things,
Believeth all things, hopeth all things,
Endureth all things
Love never faileth
And now abideth faith, hope, love
But the greatest of these are love

Of tears, the aftermarks
Of almost too much of love

Oh everyone love, as long as you can love

How sweet we roamed from field to field
And tasted all the summer's pride
Til we the royalty of love beheld
Which in the sunny beames did glide

Such a one do we remember
Whom to look upon were to love

But to see them were to love them
Love but them, and love forever
Had we never loved sae kindly
Had we never loved sae blindly
Never met—or never parted—
We had ne'er been brokenhearted

Romance of Romance

They that love beyond the world
Cannot be separated by it
Death are but crossing the world
As friends do the seas
They live in one another still

Love distill desire upon the eyes
Love bring bewitching grace into the hearts
Of those it would destroy
We pray that love may never come to us
With murderous intent
In rhythms measureless and wild
Not fires nor stars have stronger bolts
Than those sent
By the hands of the children of the gods

Alas our love you do us wrong
To cast us off discourteously
And we have loved you so long
Delighting in your company

Fair and fair and twice so fair
As fair as any may be

Love—are anterior to Life—
Posterior to Death—
Initial of Creation, and
The exponent of Earth

Down by the salley gardens
Our love and we did meet

They are not wise then
Who stand forth to buffet against Love
For love rule the gods and us

Perfect person, nobly planned
To warn, to comfort, and command

all in green went our love riding
on a great horse of gold

Love pick you up, spin you around, and
Drop you down in an unknown place
With the indifference of the tornado

Gradually our hero's shattered heart were mended.
This was their favorite:

Abide with us fast falls the eventide
The darkness deepens, love with us abide
When others fail and comforts all subside
Help of the helpless O with us abide
Swift to its close ebbs out life's little day
Earth's joys grow dim, its glories pass away
Change and decay in all the world outside
O love who changeth not in us abide

To be of courage, to hold fast. To continue the life of the knight on their own terms. They would do nothing that did not come from their own heart. They would be faithful to Rels. And perhaps—one day one day one day—love might blossom still. And if not, perhaps there were honor enough in the quest. Perhaps that were enough for a lifetime, to pursue love, even if it were never attained.

> Better to have loved and lost
> Than never to have loved at all

And the one they said most often:

> While we have breath

In the Clearing

IT WAS LATE ONE NIGHT under a thin crescent moon. Syns had wandered far from camp, quoting. They heard a strange syncopated humming. They stopped.

Human voices.

They crept closer. A clearing was filled with shadows—marching, turning in precise formations, chanting in unison:

> They are gifts far more than flowers
> Words of beauty tall as towers
> Seek ye, seek ye, feel the powers
> Powers in these words of ours

Someone shouted, "One-hundred thirteen!" The shadows moved into a new marching formation:

> We love thee and we honor thee
> We worship thee O poetry
> O Poetry we worship thee
> And do thy will
> We love thee and we love thee
> And we love thee still

Syns came nearer. The shadows were carrying rifles—no, not rifles, giant quill pens.

The same voice ordered, "Eighty-four!"

None are greater, none more high
Poetry o'ertakes the sky
Poetry shall rule someday
All shall bow down and obey

Numbers continued to be shouted and the drill team
continued to present arms and march while reciting:

There were a great poet from here
Whose muses abandoned their ear
They searched far and near
In their ale and their beer
La-lay-lu ler-lie-low le-leer

Some time later the group dispersed into the forest.
Syns returned to camp, troubled. We had thought we
were the only soul in Arcady, the only person who had
slipped outside the bounds of H-town. Now we have stumbled upon a hut in a tree, a poets' drill team. What else
disturb, illicit, these sylvan glades?

The Weeper

THE DAY AFTER THE DRILL TEAM INCIDENT Syns were still perturbed. They decided to continue rambling, now on horseback. They armored themselves but allowed Whooshes to go forth unfreighted.

It was a dappled summer afternoon with a quality of drowsy beauty. They heard what sounded like a new bird and stopped to listen. Someone were weeping.

They encountered a figure seated on boulder, clutching their foot and rocking back and forth in agony.

It was quite some time before the weeper raised their head. "Oh, hello," they finally sniffled. "We have stubbed our toe most horribly."

Syns sprang down from Whooshes to take a look. "How awful for you! We could get you some cold water from the creek."

"No, we have tried that in the past. It worsens the pain."

"Ah. We have a flask of whiskey. Might that help?"

"We cannot drink whiskey. It gives us hives."

"If you like we could take you to the hospital."

"In Normal?" A bitter laugh. "We work there! There is no help for us there!"

Syns were running out of ideas, but curious. "You work at the hospital? What do you do there, if we might ask?"

"We are the chief of psychiatry," the weeper sighed. "Ironic, aren't it?"

"We don't know what to suggest. Would you like for

us to stay with you until your pain subsides?"

"It will not subside but if you want to stay awhile, go ahead."

Our hero sat on a rock nearby.

"We know who you are," said the weeper.

"You do?"

"You are the Silver Dwarf Knight. What a charmed life you lead."

Syns could have argued the point but let it pass.

"How we envy you, we who are the unluckiest person alive. Everything are all so hopeless, especially love."

Speaking of irony, Syns thought, this sounded a lot like Jults. Also themselves, for that matter.

"We are not so selves-centered as to think we are the only one who have ever suffered in love, of course. But our case are the worst. You are probably not interested."

"Actually we are very interested."

"You see? You can be interested because you have never suffered deeply. While we have been pining for someone *our whole life*. We have done everything that could humanly be done to pursue success and then to recover from our ill luck when we failed. But nothing have ever gone right for us."

"Not one thing?"

"Not one tiny thing. Can you believe it? And lately, just when we thought our life could not get any worse, we began stumbling, stubbing our toes all the time."

"Have you thought of getting shoes of thicker leather?"

"We tried that but the leather chafed us and gave us blisters."

"Perhaps the shoes did not fit."

"We have uniquely shaped feet. No one can fit us properly."

Syns glanced down at the weeper's feet. One was shod in thin leather. The bare one looked like a normal foot, at least to their untrained eye.

"Surely there are someone somewhere who could make proper shoes for you."

"No. We tried and finally gave up. We have resigned ourselves to a lifetime of stubbed toes—at least, in the time we have left."

"But you are not old."

"We have not told you all of our diseases. Not one of them are curable."

"What are your name?"

"Not that it matters but our name are Doctor Skrimps."

"What?"

"Doctor Skrimps."

"Ah." For a moment Syns had the unpleasant thought that they shared the same name. "Pleased to meet you."

"Sadly, we cannot be pleased to meet you because we envy you so much."

"If you knew us better you wouldn't envy us."

"That are what everyone say. Everyone are so caught up in their little problems. In truth, we have never met anyone with a life as sad as ours. And don't forget we are a psychiatrist. We hear a lot of complaints."

The weeper's attitude was beginning to affect Syns, who were starting to feel gloomy, irritated, and guilty. "We find it hard to believe that nothing have ever gone right in your entire life."

"Oh, once in awhile something good happens to us, but we have learned to fear it most of all."

"Why?"

"Because it inevitably turns on us, and we are worse off than before."

"No one have ever been able to help you at all?"

"No one." There was strength and finality in the weeper's words. Such conviction was almost admirable. "Our suffering are endless."

Syns sighed and looked over at Whooshes. They wanted to be on their way. When they looked back at Skrimps they thought they saw a fleeting smile. "Well, if you're sure there is nothing we can do." They wondered, *If a weeper weep in the forest and no one are there . . .*

"Go."

Syns mounted Whooshes and abandoned the grim weeper—or were it the grinning weeper?—to their implacable misfortune.

To Sweep the Cobwebs

EARLY EVENING. Syns had ridden across the creek and gone quite far.

Now they were returning, approaching the creek from the opposite side. After their encounter with the weeper the day had been uneventful.

They came upon a copse where the trees were so tightly packed together their trunks resembled a many-shafted pillar. Syns dismounted to inspect it more closely. They walked around it; it was impenetrable from every angle.

They were about to remount when they spied a bird's nest high on a tree branch. They stretched upwards and carefully reached inside. They lifted out a silver key. Accustomed now to the ways of Arcady, they circled the copse again, looking closely for a keyhole. Returning to where they started they noticed a tiny hole in the bark of a trunk. They poked in the key. They heard a click of metal on metal and rotated their wrist. A door swung outward so quickly they had to jump back.

"Hulloo? Anyone home?" Syns called out.

They stepped into the doorway. No smell of mold or abandonment; instead, a faint smell of spices.

In the dimness they saw a table. On it were a few candles and a match tin.

They went in, lit a candle, and looked over at the walls. They were covered:

Romance of Romance

Do you know that
All the great work of the world
Is done by us?

Lives of ease are not for any persons
Nor for the gods

Hi! Ni! Ya!
Behold the persons of flint, they're us!
Four lightnings zigzag from us
Strike and return

We pray you say but two good words
What shall we do when hopes are gone?
The words leapt up like leaping swords
Sail on! Sail on! Sail on! And on!

Dawn speeds persons on their journeys
And speeds them too in their work

The frost performs its secret ministries
Unhelped by any wind

The races are over but the work is never done
While the power to work remains

These old anvils laugh
At many broken hammers

Must we be carried to the skies
On beds of ease
While others fought to win the prize
And sailed through bloody seas

Demand of us some great service, some Mohai

Establish the work of our hands upon us
Yea, the work of our hands

There were some old persons
Tossed in a blanket
Seventeen times as high as the moon
But where they were going
No mortal could tell
For under their arms they carried some brooms
Old persons, old persons, old persons, said we
Whither, ah whither, o whither go ye?
To sweep the cobwebs from the sky
And we'll be with you by and by

Death closes all: but something ere the end
Some work of noble note may yet be done
Not unbecoming those that strove with gods

O humans surely you must strive
For your salvation
A hard striving until you attain it

Romance of Romance

Work for the night is coming
Work through the morning hours
Work while the dew is sparkling
Bright on the gay spring flowers

Work when the day grows lighter
Work in the glowing sun
Work for the night is coming
When our work is done

Work for the night is coming
Under the sunset skies
While their glad tints are glowing
Work for the daylight flies

Work til the last beam fadeth
Fadeth to shine no more
Work while the night is dark'ning
When our work is o'er

    They had barely begun the first column when they
heard Whooshes neigh. Someone spoke. Syns wondered,
Could this be a wizard? And shivered.

Stranger

SYNS WHIRLED AROUND. Next to Whooshes were some-one with wild hair that swirled above their head and curled over much of their face. A large sack was slung on their back.

They looked familiar. Weren't they the strange person people referred to as the Hermit, who frequently rushed into Research, mailed stacks of letters, picked up piles more, and rushed out again? Who occasionally sat in the library, tossing books around and writing furiously? Who never spoke, except a few words to Duns in the mailroom and Livs and Lucs in the library?

"What are you doing?" A voice that crackled like one seldom used.

"Sorry to, um, trespass." It occurred to Syns, too late, that a knight did not apologize.

"You are searching for us. Why?"

"We weren't." Syns' fingers went to the velvet pouch, visible on a cord around their neck. "At least not on purpose. We're just a poor lonely knight."

"The Silver Dwarf. We heard them talking about you over at the library. Too bad . . ."

"'Too bad' what?"

"Never mind. You want to step aside so we can enter our own home?"

"Sorry."

The Hermit moved candles and tin and set the sack

on the table. The room held both of them with little space to spare. "So you took the pouch."

"It has been a great comfort. But of course it is yours." Syns began to remove it.

"Keep it. We don't want it. You're in love, we suppose."

"Yes."

"Gods help you then. A terrible distraction from work."

"Perhaps being in love *are* our work."

"Of course you would say that."

"But we have read the sayings. Surely you were in love once."

"Yes."

"What happened?"

A pause. "We renounced it but it were too lonely. We have a new love now."

"Ah. From afar?"

"No. They are here with us."

Syns looked around the cramped room. "Where?"

The Hermit sighed. "We will introduce you. They would wish it. Follow us."

The Rock

THE HERMIT LIFTED A LANTERN from under the table, lit it, and opened a door at the back of the room. They entered an even smaller room. No one were there but the walls bore further writings:

> And there are a capacity of vice
> To make your blood creep

> Evil be ye my good

> In starting and waging a war
> It are not right that matter but victory

> Do what you will

> Power are the supreme law

> Better to reign in hells than serve in heavens

> Come ye spirits
> And fill us from the crown to the toe
> Top-full of direst cruelty!
> Make thick our blood

Things were getting decidedly creepy. Syns heard the scratch and smelled the sulfur of a match being ignited.

The room was small for the drawing of even a dagger, and far too far from help.

"Why don't you turn around so we can introduce you properly?" said the Hermit.

Syns did, their hand on the hilt of their dagger anyway. The Hermit had lit several candles next to what appeared to be a small altar.

On it was an ordinary-looking rock which the Hermit seemed to be addressing. "We have a visitor, dearest. The Silver Dwarf, a poor knight in the throes of love." They turned to Syns. "This are Glyphs."

"Um, pleased to meet you." Best to humor the lunatic.

"They are pleased to meet you as well, and invite you to have dinner with us."

"Well . . ."

"Please. They love guests and you are our first."

"Ych. Okay." Going along with the gag.

"Perhaps you would like to tend to your horse while we make preparations."

Escape! "Excellent idea."

Back in the evening air Syns jumped on Whooshes and sped away. But then they slowed. This was not the way of the brave knight. "Buddies, we're going back. If you hear us yell, come over and start kicking at the door, okay?"

They returned to the copse. A savory smell emanated from the open door of the hut.

Syns tended to Whooshes and watered and fed them

with oats from the supply bag. They remembered their emergency flask of whiskey. Though they no longer drank spirits, more or less, this seemed a good time to take a salutary gulp. They took several, then tucked the flask inside their breastplate.

The Hermit poked their head out. "Dinner is served." The kitchen was transformed. Candles glowed, a vase of wildflowers sat upon an embroidered cloth on the table, and a box served for a second chair. The rock was on the table. "Sit there," said the Hermit.

Syns had the only eating bowl as well as the only normal-sized spoon. The Hermit had the cooking pan and cooking spoon. By the rock were a tiny plate and spoon.

"Very nice," said Syns. "But we never remove our visor, even to dine. Do you have a straw?"

"We'll get you one. Keep Glyphs company." The Hermit dashed outside.

Syns wondered how to make small talk. "Nice weather lately." How absurd. Rocks undoubtedly had entirely different attitudes toward such things.

The Hermit returned with a cut reed which worked brilliantly.

Dinner was a delicious stew. Their mug contained water. When Syns offered whiskey the Hermit pointed to an admonition on the wall:

Spirits make us believe great things
Are easily accomplished. They lie

"But you are free to drink, Silver Dwarf. They paused and bent their head toward the rock. Glyphs would like a drop too."

Syns poured, literally, a drop of whiskey into a thimble. "Cheers."

"Thank you. Glyphs asked if you know any jokes."

Syns told the few jokes they could recall and the meal became rather jolly.

After dinner the Hermit wanted to spend a bit of time alone with Glyphs. "But we would both like for you to stay. Then you and we could converse some more."

The First Circle

THE NIGHT WAS BEAUTIFUL, starlit with a parenthesis of moon. Syns checked on Whooshes, who were fast asleep.

After awhile the Hermit came outside. They sat on adjacent tree-roots at the edge of the creek.

"We never drink," said the Hermit, "but tonight shall be an exception if there's anything left in your flask."

They passed the flask back and forth and listened to the night sounds: Whooshes breathing, bugs chirping, branches rustling, the creek muttering to itself.

"We are grateful to you," said the Hermit.

"To us?"

"For the kindness you have shown to Glyphs. They are pleased with you. Also, we know that it were you who slew the Komodos. Even here it disturbed our concentration."

"Oh. Well."

They sat awhile, sipping.

"We are grateful to you also," said Syns. "For the pouch. It saved us." Suddenly our lonely knight poured out the story of what had happened at the castle, from meeting their beloved, to the fan, to the unhappy kiss.

The Hermit stretched out on the tree-root and looked up at the stars. "We too had an unhappy love. For awhile it were good and we thought it would last forever. But it were too consuming. We had too many devotions, our love and our work. Try as we might, we could not attend to them all. We felt like we were going mad. Finally we had to leave. For awhile we had neither love nor work. We lived in the tiny hut you found, wrote on the walls, and suffered. Then one day we were free. We left the hut of sorrow and came here and made this hut of work. We knew we were finished with love forever." A long pause. "But . . . love found us again. And now, finally, we have everything. It are very difficult. But we manage."

"Were your prior love—if you don't mind us asking—a human being?"

The Hermit took a big gulp and sighed. "Yes. Their name were Jults."

Syns sputtered and lost a mouthful of whiskey. The Hermit were the jilter! The jilter of Jults! "But how could you . . . how could you bear to leave?"

"Oooohhh!" The Hermit wailed like a coyote. "We are divided! There can never be a solution. We have Glyphs now, who do not require quite so much of us. Perhaps it would be better if we did not love at all but we are not strong enough. We left Jults because we knew our fallibility. We cannot let ourselves be derailed again." Another long pause. "Do you know Jults?"

"Yes."

"Do you know how they have fared since we left?"

"Well, for your information—" Syns stopped. "No, we don't know." After a pause, "What was your work?" Part of them wanted to understand the reason for the disturbing sayings in the second room; part of them were afraid to find out.

"At the time, when we met Jults, we were a professor for a correspondence university. We also taught a couple of courses at the little college that used to be in Old N. We wrote. Essays, articles."

"And now? What is it you do? All that mail back and forth—"

"You wouldn't understand."

"Were Jults your first love?"

"No. There were one before."

Sympathy for the Pedophile

"WE WERE THREE YEARS OLD," said the Hermit after a few gulps of whiskey. "Our parents were professors and told us the truth about everything at all times. They told us we were an H and nothing could be done about it. We were lonely. Perhaps because we knew.

"And then a child moved in next door, also three. A smiling happy child, Chims. We met one day on the sidewalk. We informed them we were an H. We felt we had to warn them. They said perhaps they were an H too, they would go ask their parents. They came back and said they were! We became friends. One day we held hands as we walked around in our back yard. It was the happiest moment of our life. The sun turned everything golden yellow, as beautiful as lemon drops."

A long silence. Syns said, "A poignant story."

"To this day it was the happiest moment of our life. Shortly thereafter Chims' family moved away. We were bereft. We didn't think of getting their address. We felt miserable and helpless.

"Ten years later, when we were thirteen, we looked up their family in the phone book. They were just across town. How stupid that we had never thought of it before. We took the bus and met at a tiny park full of litter and bird droppings. We sat together on top of a picnic table. We felt nothing except loss for what could never again be. Pass me the flask.

"They did not feel the same way. We talked about that day in the back yard. They remembered it when we reminded them. They said it was a happy day for them too. But it was merely a memory. They were seeing someone who were thirteen. They said we could start meeting if we wanted to. They even took our hand.

"We felt nothing. The sun was sullen. The houses were faded. We were so distraught we told our parents when we got home. We told them everything, about the golden sun in the back yard and the ugly light in the park. It was a mistake.

"They sent us to a psychologist. Even before H-town we saw a psychologist. They tried to show us how wrong we were to be wishing we were three years old holding hands with a three year old child. How we needed to act our age. The treatment failed. We pretended to be cured, finally, because the whole thing were so horrible. After that we told no one.

"But even now we yearn for that day so long ago. Sometimes we dream of a happy child and we feel drawn to them. Do you understand? We feel drawn. We wake up and wonder, What if we were to hold hands, would the bright sun finally shine?"

"And Jults?"

"We tried, you know. But . . ."

"But the sun did not turn everything golden yellow."

"No."

"And you never explained."

A long time passed while they looked at the sky. "There were someone—something else, before Glyphs. We loved a gecko. They were very young. But they died of a rare disease after a few months. We grieved and thought we would never love again. Now, for the first time, our love are far older than we are."

"The rock."

"Yes. Glyphs. We were too upset about being a pedophile, if that are what we are. So we forced ourselves to love a rock. And Glyphs are very sturdy, very self-sufficient. A bit uncompromising but we manage."

It seemed to Syns that they were supposed to say something. "We see," they lied. It were all quite disturbing. Their passion for Rels were seeming healthier by the minute.

The Hermit continued, "Desire and identity. Falling in love suddenly tell us who we are. Falling is the right word. You do not plan it. Something are unleashed. *You are this!* You can be completely surprised.

"Society have its methods for roping identity into something acceptable; it mock you and try to shame you into having a more normal love, a more normal identity.

"A human can be in love with anything. It can be true love. A fetish can be true love. Did you know that? It are not pedophilia to be drawn to children *if you are a child*. But later it are horrifically wrong. But what if you are? What are you supposed to do, kill yourselves?" The Hermit were ramping up.

"The loves of the human, so unruly, despite culture's

myriad structures to control them. All the churches and creeds and parables and lessons, and psychotherapy. With the result that the truths go underground. They become secrets. So much humiliation and sense of wrong over these things.

"What if you were the leader of a cult and you were in love with your followers and they were in love with you. Where are the harm? Society say, 'It are terrible, you will be smitten down.' Perhaps you will. And perhaps you won't. It are not always from criminality that we love what are socially deemed unacceptable.

"Sometimes we simply love without knowing why; feel lost and estranged, even with ourselves. Sin and wrong, shame and misery, all the secrets confessed and unconfessed, all the loves requited and not, all the lovers furtive and apart, all the confusion and defiance.

"Who *are* we who love this and not this, whose love are outside the fenced yard of what is acceptable, holy, good, and mentionable. Are that not the heart also? Can we find no resting place except in our encyclopedia of deviance?

"The truth are not so simple. Perversion, you say. Obsession, you say. It are wrong, you say. A travesty, you say. Have people take truth serum and then take your polls. What shall you find? The imagination, the dreams, the labyrinths of desire and longing. These are our human romance. These are what cannot be enacted. Or spoken. Or written. Or published. Almost, they cannot be thought."

Darkside of Romance

SYNS AND THE HERMIT TALKED far into the night. Syns rarely enjoyed listening to anyone for very long; they became restless and stopped paying attention. But it felt good to be talking with the Hermit, who, odd though they were, listened intently and responded passionately. Nothing was neutral or irrelevant. They had probably been a great teacher.

"Do you think romance can be a path of enlightenment?" asked Syns.

"We don't know what enlightenment are. Romance, surrender to feeling, passionate intuition, can be big mistakes. You saw the walls in the second room. But reason are fallible too."

"Those walls are warnings?"

"Of course. What else would they be?"

Syns felt considerably relieved. "What of other pursuits beside being in love? What of the passionate pursuit of science, of the arts, of knowledge?"

"There is a commonly held idea that if you do not feel confident that you can accomplish something, but make an effort toward it anyway, then the endeavor is therapeutic, even admirable. Let us consider. What if you don't feel confident you can be a dictator, yet you try. Are that admirable? What if you want to play the lute but feel inadequate. You struggle and eventually master it but you forget to feed your pets. What if you passionately desire to be a philanthropist and found hospitals for the needy but you neglect your own family. Culture say it is okay to have passions as long as they are directed toward acceptable things and do not override your other obligations."

"But isn't that correct?"

"There are no correctness. It are just a matter of judgment and cultural fashion. For a long time now, moderation has been the template. But it was not always so. Extremities of passion were once considered higher spiritual states. Were they only primitive desires, the ids dressed up to look like things of more value?"

"But how are we to know if our passions are worthwhile?"

"As we indicated, there are two problems: the object of the passion and the degree of abandonment to it. We've been speaking of both. Fools in love tend to be forgiven. It happen to everyone more or less—they become useless for awhile. We have almost forgiven ourselves. But what if passion never abate and become obsession?"

"What is the cure?"

"We are no expert. All we know are that we surround ourselves with exhortations and warnings and work hard every day."

"Speaking of passion, we encountered something in these very woods last night." Syns described their encounter with the poets' drill team.

"What alarmed you about them?"

"It wasn't the poetry, which was merely bad. It was

the precision, the militaristic quality. And the leader shouting out numbers and being obeyed unquestioningly."

The Hermit sighed. "We don't suppose . . . never mind. A lovesick knight are of no use."

They sat awhile not speaking. The moon had set. The sky was a black liquid effervescing with stars.

Finally the Hermit roused themselves. They invited Syns to stay over and have breakfast in the morning if they didn't mind sleeping outside. They went in and Syns wandered over to Whooshes.

Equinophilia

Whooshes stood sleeping, their dark coat awash with starlight.

"Noble being," whispered Syns. They ran their hand along the mane, feeling the coarseness and vibrancy of the cascading hair.

"So beautiful. So wise."

Our knight were flooded with love. They gazed upon the great eyelids fimbriated with long lashes. They reached out to caress the face. They placed their head against the neck, armor against warmth, breathing against nickering, in deep communion.

They pushed up their visor, brushed lips across muzzle.

"Ah, you are so much more than we deserve." They lay down nearby, carried rapidly away in currents of sleep. "And so much better than a rock."

Suicide Music

SOMETIME IN THE NIGHT WHOOSHES HAD LAIN down next to our hero. Syns awoke early with their arm flung across the equine neck.

There was a divine smell of breakfast in the air. They sat up. The hut door was wide open and Syns could see bustling within. The Hermit poked their head out. "Come and get it."

The table was set as before with fresh flowers, and Glyphs at their place of honor. Syns' bowl was full of steaming porridge with honey, wild berries, and pieces of sausage in it, small enough to be sucked up through the reed.

Syns had a great sense of well-being: they had the beauty of the world, the company of friends, the blessing of a quick imagination, the hope of love.

After breakfast the Hermit produced a guitar. "It has been a long time since we sang. But Glyphs enjoy it and we feel very good this morning."

Music too.

Their host tuned the guitar, strummed a few chords, and sang. Their voice had changed overnight: it was strong and sonorous.

The words were of hopeless love. Syns began to weep.

The dances and festival music of Old M were enjoyable and harmless. But there was a type of H-music that was sad and ultra-romantic. It had always overwhelmed Syns. Once heard, it would repeat endlessly in their mind. To themselves they called it tearjerker suicide music. It stole into the ears like hemlock.

The Hermit gazed worshipfully upon the rock as they sang.

Syns wept harder. Their heart were breaking, flooded with longing so intense it were unbearable. Down and down they sank until they were at their lowest point, far lower than the kiss.

They no longer wanted to live. They would commit suicide and put and end to their intolerable quest for impossible love.

Somewhere beyond the forest were the dunes, then the waiting arms of the sea—*those* arms would not spurn them.

They kissed the sleeping Whooshes. "Goodbye, buddies. Sorry."

The Hermit continued to sing while they left.

Extreme Unction

THE UNDERGROWTH was becoming thicker, with nodding sedge, tearthumb, the occasional stand of cattails. There were sweet scents in the air: high bush blueberry, purple boneset, rue.

Suddenly their foot was submerged beneath chartreuse water. The swamp. They had forgotten it.

Soon the water was halfway up their steel-plated thighs, their feet sinking deeply into the swamp's muddy bottom. They were in a sort of trance, reduced to the single act of walking in a straight line except when forced to go around the moss-laden trees—red maple, black gum, sweet gum—and floating logs.

The water was almost to their navel. They moved in the algal universe: bladderwort, floating mud-plantain, water lilies. It would not be long now. A bitter laugh. They were a failure at everything, even a dignified death. The swamp would tell no tales.

Swampwater was up to their chest. They could barely go forward. Should they stop? Sit down and drown? No. They would struggle until they could go no more.

They looked down as they pressed on, watching their grave rise higher. Farewell to this sad and pointless life.

They slammed into something and raised their heavy head.

The Face of the Sublime

THE LIGHT WAS DIMMED BY TREES and their trailing festoons of moss. At first nothing could be differentiated in this world of green upon green.

Eventually they discerned a rock in front of them, sloping upwards a few feet above the water. The slime on its lower surface gave way to lichens above. The rock extended into the gloom in both directions. To continue they would have to climb over it.

Syns tried to scale the rock but repeatedly slipped back. Was this, then, how it was to end?

They paused awhile. Not yet. They had an appointment with the sea. Of necessity they removed their armor and flung it up onto the rock.

There was no purchase on the rock's slick stratum but they finally managed to haul themselves up to the lichens. They lay panting, arm muscles in agony. They stood. The rock sloped back much farther than they had expected. They walked ahead. And stopped in amazement.

They were not on a rock at all, but on a granite escarpment which dropped down into a deep valley.

The valley was filled with trees, much taller than Arcady forest. Some trees were so tall they rose higher than those in the swamp.

Syns zigzagged their way down.

Matchless solitude. No mark to indicate that anyone had been here before. They were the first, delivered unto something more primeval, more fundamental, than the sorrows and joys of love; they were delivered unto beauty itself. They gazed upon the face of the sublime.

Syns did not believe in magic, but this was the closest they had ever come to feeling a presence. This valley was theirs—not to own or to keep, but to receive.

They wandered under the canopy of trees: trunks smooth and rough, in shades from near-white to near-black, branches narrow and wide, coniferous and leafy, some bearing nuts, some holding acorns, some in the embrace of wild grapevines. Beneath were flowering and fruited trees.

A creek trickled through the valley bottom. Syns followed its ferny banks, recognizing beech drops, horse-balm, and lion's foot. They came to a place where the forest backed away and they were in a meadow of twisted and panic grass, lupine, goldenrod, blue-curls, fleabane, dark berries of blue cohosh, harebells, field thistle, blackberry, huckleberry.

They bathed in the clear water of the creek. They lay down in the meadow to dry in the sun. Bugs and bees droned, butterflies flitted, birds chattered.

In relief and contentment at being alive in the warm prickly grass, they looked up at the brilliant cerulean sky, the pristine carraran clouds.

Battle

LIONS LIE SIDE BY SIDE in a long row. White manes flow around watchful heads. More arrive below, above.

They rise up, stand on mountains of hind legs. Unhurried bodies lunge. Jaws open, bite, devour. Claws extend, scourge.

They fall. Rise again, whole.

The Great Battle of the Lions in the Sky. Mute armies fight to a death that is no death, to a victory that is the pure thrall of exultant power, the pure joy of resplendent beauty.

The warriors are leaner now. Redness tints the field. Gold for glory.

All sink down. Ambiguous, complete.

Civil Engineering

SYNS DRANK WATER FROM THE CREEK, ate blackberries and hickory nuts.

They missed Whooshes.

They went back to the escarpment and climbed up. How easy it was to move without armor, almost like floating. They reached the summit, crossed over to the swamp, and lowered themselves in.

Before they were halfway across they heard a familiar whinny. A short while later a welcome form came into view, pawing at the edge of the swamp.

"Buddies!"

Syns mounted and urged their companion into the water. But for once the horse balked. "It's okay. It isn't dangerous." But Whooshes would not go.

"Alright. We'll think of something."

They rode back to their camp in Arcady. They gathered everything, armored the horse and loaded the supplies onto them. They returned to the edge of the swamp. It was fairly dark now; they lit their lantern. While their companion watched, Syns went into the water alone.

They found two thick short logs of equal length and upended them, creating swampy stepping stones. Whooshes were willing to assist, putting a front foot onto each log, driving them down into the muddy bottom. Syns found two more logs, slightly longer, and set them just beyond the first pair. Whooshes stood on these as well, sinking them as far as they would go. After countless hours they completed a causeway across the swamp. The tops of the logs were just below the water's rim, invisible. But the horse knew the depth and location of each one and walked across, unerring.

When they reached the other side, Whooshes stepped easily onto the rock. Syns saw a bulky shape on the granite. Their armor. They would abandon it. No, they would throw it into the swamp. Finally they lashed it with the supplies.

The velvet pouch lay on the lichens. Syns heaved it into the swamp. Their days of love were over. They were not able; their feelings ran too deep. They would live out their days in simple toil.

Making wide switchbacks, horse and rider descended into the valley, their way faintly lit by the evangel of dawn.

They made camp in the meadow and slept.

Waking, Syns' muscles clamored for more labor.

Nearby was the tallest tree in the valley. They looked up into its branches which began far above. They made a ladder, twelve-runged, and scrambled upward.

They were in the branches. Higher and higher they climbed. The rim of the valley sank beneath their view. The sea rose up.

It took three days of intense effort. They wove ropes from grasses. They collected thick straight branches. They slung the ropes over the tree-limbs, which served as axles for lifting. Whooshes were master of drayage and obedient counterweight for the pulleys.

When finished, a treehouse nested high above. It was a simple platform to which Syns secured their tarps and put down their sleeping bags. They made a shelter for Whooshes at the base of the tree and filled it with dried grass from the meadow.

They brought more dried grass up to the treehouse for a fragrant mattress.

And the Morning

THE EDGE OF THE SLEEPING BAG, olive green canvas. Next to it the edge of the tarp, heavier canvas, darker olive. A brass grommet almost black in its grooved inner circle, through which loops gray-white cotton rope. The rope, taut, crosses over three of the branches of the platform. The first branch: gray-brown bark, deeply corrugated lengthwise, softer undulations across. Shadows in the grooves. A spot of dried mud. The next branch: slightly thinner, smoother, the color lighter, gray-tan. The third branch, the farthest over: thicker, pure gray, smooth, a nub where a side-branch was removed, yellow-white wood exposed.

After traversing the platform the rope wraps around a branch of the tree—stout, almost black—two times. It is knotted, the ends hang several feet beneath, curving slightly in empty space.

Past the ends, the tops of trees in the valley, in shades of gray-green, blue-green, beige, brown.

Behind, an arc of the valley's blue-gray stone.

Beyond, white sparkle of ocean.

Opposing View

WHAT WAS THE VIEW in the opposite direction? They rolled over. The tallest aspects of H-town rose above the treetops of Arcady: the tips of the Komodos, the penthouse of H-town Publishing, and, highest of all, the upper region of the tower. Something was odd about the tower but they turned away.

The valley was their new life. Their old love were not welcome.

Spiders

THE NEXT DAY TRAITOROUS EYES glanced at the tower.

Upwards from its roof were two extensions like masts of a ship. Between them a rigging resembling shrouds and rattlings was suspended. Two things were crawling on it like spiders on a web. One of them—even at this distance Syns knew—were Rels.

Bright lights flashed. Sunlight on steel. The spiders scuttled this way and that. Sword-fighting.

There was but one answer to all questions concerning Rels: they were mad.

Our hero slammed their eyelids shut, too late to avert a jolt of pain to their foolish foolish heart.

La Chute

SPIDER-PIRATES WERE FIGHTING on their web-rigging the next morning. A spider fell: Rels. Syns were already in motion, shot through with terror.

They raced down from the treehouse. Their armor—ticket into the castle—was in a heap on the ground. They jumped in. No time for barding. They saddled Whooshes and tore off across the valley, up the escarpment, over the causeway, and through Arcady.

A feeling expanded from the chest to the neck and throat: desire that were not about their own need but merely frightened, certain, purposeful. They would give their life, without question.

Rescue

A CROWD HAD GATHERED at the castle and were increasing, mostly Rels' fan club members. A few held lighted candles even though it was day.

Had they died then?

Syns felt nothing but compassion, joined in sorrow. When the fans saw Silvers a weak cheer went up. The castle guards were keeping everyone out, but with whispers of "Tels' champion" they allowed Syns through.

They leapt from their horse. "Where are they?"

"In the tower, our liege."

"Are they . . . are they . . ."

"Banged up, our liege."

Syns did not believe it. "Take me to them at once."

"Of course."

"Hurry, hurry, run, damn 'em." Syns' resolve desperately parried the visions their imagination kept trying to let in. "While we have breath, while we have breath."

Once in the tower our hero ran up the stairs and pounded on the door. "Open up for the Silver Dwarf!" The door opened and they burst in.

The court were there. "Take us to the Sovereign!" Syns shouted.

Tels led them through the door behind the throne and down a corkscrew-steep circular staircase. They went through a doorway into a chamber where Rels were lying in a canopied bed. A doctor were hovering over them. In a chair next to the bed sat Cyras.

"*Rels! Speak to us!*" Syns' voice was a sob. They flung themselves to their knees.

"Ah, Silver Dwarf Knight. Ye return as suddenly as ye depart." Rels had extended a hand, and was . . . smiling.

"You—you are alright?"

"Bruised, scraped, possibly knocked unconscious for a moment, but otherwise fine."

The doctor looked at Syns and frowned. "Have you any influence with the Sovereign?"

"Influence? What do you mean?"

"We've been trying to get their highness to go to the hospital for x-rays but they refuse."

Syns turned to Rels. "You refuse?"

"Yes."

"And of course we have no influence."

"Ye have our appreciation."

Syns said to the doctor, "They are impossible." Our knight were giddy, relief had made them weak. They rose, then sank back to the floor, where they sat with their legs sprawled in front of them. "What . . . happened?"

"We were in a competition, the fight for the title. It is a new sport, in which sword-fighting is done—"

"We saw it. What *happened*?"

"We made an unfortunate lunge and lost our balance. Then, instead of dropping our sword we held onto it, and cut the rigging as we fell. Of course we forfeited the tournament. It were entirely our own fault."

"And what happened?"

"We fell into the safety net, but we cut that too, and fell further, about ten more feet to the roof of the Tower. Which is why we got bruised."

With comprehension came the stirrings of the old complaint. How *could* you not realize how loved you are, how necessary for the survival of so many. Such impossible, damnable blindness.

Chastanea Antigua

THE DOCTOR AND TELS went out.

"As we weren saying, Rels, about the October—"

Rels interrupted, "Oh, Silver Dwarf Knight, have ye met Cyras the Giant, our knight?"

Our knight? *Our knight?!* Jealousy zapped through Syns like a high voltage current.

"Cyras, here are the Silver Dwarf Knight, champion to Tels."

Cyras nodded curtly. "We metten."

Rels chuckled. "Oh yea, we had forgotten. When all the brave knights ganged up on one."

The breath and vocal cords of Cyras were foisting sound waves upon the air again. "Ye aren most astonishingly fortunate to have a sponsor such as Tels. Pray telleth us, what aren your plans with regard to them?"

"Plans?"

Rels interposed. "The Silver Dwarf Knight are very humble, Cyras, something ye would know nothing about. They don't like to talk about their accomplishments or plans, and above all they despise being admired or pursued."

"We shallen force ourselves to refrain."

Syns were struggling frantically not to surrender to despair. While we have breath, while we have breath.

Rels said, "We have not heard of any new exploits since ye left us so suddenly. Tell us, what have ye been doing?"

Trying to forget about you. "Uh . . . tending to our horse." The chasm between them were unbridgeable. Syns were weeping. If this behemoth are right for you, then we are not. If you are right for this mastodon, then you are not right for us. But if you want someone like *us* then we are the ideal choice, for we are the best example of ourselves there are.

"Will ye be staying with us awhile?"

"Um." Fighting that special form of exhaustion and failure—fighting, fighting. O Sovereign, why are you giving them another chance? Did the turn mean nothing to you? At least you are still in the tower. Perhaps Cyras were banned until now.

". . . will ye do it?"

"What?"

"Cyras and we were talking about the Harvest Festival, coming up on the first of October. It is the last outdoor celebration of the year. Would ye be interested in taking part?"

Headlong. The life of the knight. "Okay."

"We just hadden an idea," said Cyras. "Ye aren new here. Shallen we engage against each other?"

"Engage?"

"Allez allez allez."

Joust with Cyras. The life of the knight. "Why not?"

Rels grinned. "Excellent."

Cyras stood. They glanced at Syns. "Well, then, we willen see yow at the tourney."

Syns rose also. Next to the giant they were incontestably a dwarf. Not in the mood to look up, they stared at the surcoated acreage of chest in front of them. "See you."

Cyras bent down and kissed the Sovereign on the brow. "We han an appointment but we willen check in on yow later." They went out.

The Sovereign were suddenly petulant. "You fled!"

"You fell!"

Rels laughed. "Then perhaps we are even."

Suddenly there was an unworldly noise in the air, a deafening syncopation like a blender come down from the gods.

"Fear not!" shouted Syns. Our hero were out the door, sword drawn, ready to meet the gargantuan appliance and slay it in its tracks.

Blending In

A DRAWN SWORD WAS A MISTAKE in the narrow staircase. They held it above their head like a tatar while they ascended. They dashed across the tower room and joined the throng that were rushing down the main staircase. Partway, a side door stood open and the mob were pushing through.

They were on the roof of the castle hall, just inside the wall walk. A helicopter was landing less than ten yards away. Syns shoved their way to the front of the crowd. The sword undoubtedly added to their authority.

A set of steps unfolded from the side of the machine. Two tall figures emerged.

"This way." The doctor had elbowed their way forward. Swiftly they escorted the arrivals through the door into the tower. The court and Syns pursued.

Back in the tower room, Tels put a hand on Syns' vambrace. "Rels' parents. They will want some time alone with their child."

Doctor and parents went through the door behind the throne. Syns paced.

Nothing happened for a long time. The court drifted away and Syns were alone. Finally the doctor emerged and then puffed out the main door.

At last the parents appeared. One of them called out irritably, "Say there, we could sure use a couple of martinis. Maybe a bucket."

Syns sprang forward. "We'd be glad to assist."

"*Must* we wait here? This place is so dark and dank and horrible."

"Follow us." Syns' last stay in the castle had been limited, but they had not forgotten their youthful labors and visits. They led the parents down to the screen passage by the front doors, and along it, arriving at the great hall. They opened an arched door to a tiny room on the left, the Hornets' Butts.

The bartender were alone, polishing tankards. "Gils, at your service."

"Martinis," ordered our knight.

"Join us," a parent commanded Syns.

The people who knew Rels best. "We would love to."

Time passed and drinks were drunk. At one point Gils set down hot pasties on a silver tray.

Syns learned that a martini sucked through a pewter straw could be as cold and life-altering as any other but the olive was out of the question.

They learned that the parents owned a corporation, Whirlee, which included newspapers, advertising and publicity firms, magazines, television stations, a movie studio, and a chain of theme parks. H-town was ripe for takeover; it had a massive untapped income potential; the current financial structure was horribly backward and politically suspect; with restructuring, H-town could be ready for public offering on short order, there were already interested investors; "targeted development" was the keyword.

At some point Gils were ordered to "Just put a bottle and a bucket of ice on the table" and dismissed.

"No offense, Dwarfie—you don't mind if we call you that, do you?—but we know how much you make and you have to agree that on the outside your job would command far less. Not saying you're one of those shirkers, but face it, H-town is a haven for 'em. The time has come to bring this place out from its financial fantasy life and into the marketplace. Even if you were promoted to, say, an executive secretary—which, by the way, you might be good at, and we might be interested in pursuing it with you—still, you know, it makes no sense that you would earn the same as a CEO."

"Well, you know, once we—"

"Bet you were a cute little pasty-maker or a decorative little blacksmith."

"Actually—" for a moment Syns had the impulse to reveal the truth. They caught themselves just in time. "Guess you might have a point."

"Don't be offended. We're plain-speaking folks. And we're not prejudiced. We *want* people to better themselves. With education you could go far. Have you considered night school? We like you. You know your way outside a martini. And the Silver Dwarf bit—great gimmick. So is keeping that visor down all the time. Say, how would you like to be our personal attendant while we're here?"

"Love to."

Later, three dinners were delivered, one drinkable, along

with more ice and another bottle. Later still, Syns staggered off to their chamber and were felled onto the bed.

There was a knock and Glurs' voice saying, "Are ye awake, our liege?"

"Uh." Our hero struggled toward coherence. "What time is it?"

"Two in the afternoon, our liege. The Sovereign's parents are asking for you. They have asked you to join them for breakfast."

"Whooshes are okay?"

"Just fine, our liege."

Syns considered the situation. The parents like us. They're from a different planet of privilege but so are Rels. We have completely different—okay, opposing—values. Always have. Maybe that's long enough. We're in love now. Things change. There probably *ought* to be a limit to what you were willing to sacrifice for love. But were there? Hearts go where they go, rightly or wrongly. Yes we know we're rationalizing. So what? Through all cultures, all time, lovers do what they have to do. Why should we be different? So what if Rels are a corporate criminal? They can always do good deeds through philanthropy. Anyway what's wrong with making H-town more profitable? It *is* out-of-date. They aren't trying to get rid of it, just bring it into the contemporary business world.

"Okay, we're getting up."

Fragrant from a quick bath, in clean garments and

attendant-polished armor, they set out with a light step. First order of business, a quick visit with Rels. Glurs were outside the door. "Take us to the tower."

"The Sovereign are not seeing anyone except their parents, our liege."

"Are they alright?"

"Yea, just fatigued. Today they wish only to rest."

Syns were momentarily disappointed. "On to the parents then."

"They await you in the ruin."

The were led down the hallway away from the tower. Up a staircase. Out a door. They emerged into a captower on the roof. To their left was the gleaming surface of the helicopter, directing brutal shafts of light into Syns' eyes.

In front of them was the ruin. Kriks had designed it to look like an ancient tower that had fallen into disrepair, with jagged walls of loose stones.

They entered and were blinded. Glass had been set into the spaces between the stones, the ceiling was one big skylight. The room was painted white, the floor was a marble-like paving of white and gold.

The parents were wearing dark glasses. "Dwarfie! Come. Sit. Gin fizzes and sausages. Pull up a straw."

Syns plopped down in a chair.

"We learned something about you, you little fox."

Fear. "Oh?"

"One of the *reasons* it's quiet is because of you! We hadn't heard that that horror of a rollercoaster was finally put out of its misery. We salute you!" They lifted their fizzes. And, you sneaky little fox, we know your other secret, too."

Fear again.

"You're Tels' knight. Not bad for a dwarf."

"Thanks."

"So modest. Just what we're always talking about. All this whining about handicaps. All you have to do is set your mind on something and you can overcome anything. Just look at you. Keep it up, you'll do fine."

Syns sipped breakfast and wondered how to shift the conversation to Rels. They did not have to worry.

"This medieval business has gotten way out of hand. Like this sword-fighting nonsense. If you've got an ear with Rels you've got to emphasize that it must stop. We've got much better plans."

"What, uh, are they?"

"Okay, listen. First of all it's obvious that Rels is quite extraordinarily beauti—"

"*Handsome*, dammit—"

"Yeah, yeah. Sorry, Dwarfie, we always argue about this—you know, the, uh, sex of our child. Anyway, Rels will be the face of the new park. In fact, we're thinking of calling it Whirlee-Rels. Nice ring to it, don't you think? We don't want some freakish-looking H that would scare people off. And you've got to admit Rels looks like royalty and already *is*! Talk about luck! That's another thing that has to change, this crazy rule of having people stay at their jobs for only a year or until someone else wants it. The business community has to be able to relate. Anyway, with Rels being such a great-looking representative, we can do a tip-top advertising campaign. So what do you think?"

"Tip-top."

"Another thing fits in with this. We think it's time Rels settled down with someone. That giant just isn't right for the image. We're thinking non-H, someone from the entertainment industry. Recognizable." The parents looked at each other. "One little thing we haven't resolved yet. We disagree on what the person should be. The sex problem again. You have an opinion, Dwarfie?"

"Um, well—"

"Anyway, it's high time Rels came to a decision. Get some children in the picture. Helps the image and the bottom line."

Children? These people were in their own F-town, F for fantasy. Syns found a mustard seed of courage. "Don't you think it should be up to Rels to decide whom they want to be with?"

"Don't misunderstand us. It's not like we'd ever think of forcing Rels into anything. We'd present options."

"Well, but what if Rels *want* to be with an H?"

"You mean that giant—"

"Absolutely not the giant. Total agreement with you there. But what about an H who were, say, wealthy and successful."

"Possibly. But not just wealthy and successful. You'd

have to add photogenic and *famous*."

Could we do it? Could we go back to writing? Do it on the outside like we'd been offered? What about screenplays? The parents would undoubtedly love it if Syns starred in a movie. While we have breath.

Syns slurped several fizzes in rapid succession. If we do it we definitely have to go back to drinking.

"What are you thinking about, Dwarfie? We know that crafty little mind is up to something."

"We're thinking about everything you said. Aside from the part about taking up with a non-H, it sounds good."

"We want something better for Rels. Every parent does."

"Well, you're not H's."

The parents exchanged another glance. "Just between us, we are. But we don't flaunt it."

"So Rels are—"

"Adopted, of course. We got into a pilot project for H's to adopt H's. Best thing that ever happened to us."

What? H's adopting? Syns were thunderstruck but trying to recover. "We don't think you should take away their choices, that's all we're saying."

"We like your style, Dwarfie. You're not afraid to speak your mind. We just might have a place for you at Whirlee. How would you like that?"

"That might be good, depending."

"Sly little fox." Everyone laughed.

The parents asked Syns to give them a guided tour of H-town. Future-town was a disaster. The whole thing needed to be torn down and rebuilt with state-of-the-art rides and amusements. A group was standing next to the Komodos. A parent went up to find out what was going on. When they learned it was to ascertain the best way to dismantle the rollercoasters, they slapped Dwarfie on the back and complimented them all over again. The zoo was a joke. The whole thing was so uninspired and unsanitary it was a wonder F-town made any money at all.

Old Normal was outdated and a waste of time. Everything there could be incorporated into New Normal. It should have a theme, too, maybe something related to patriotism.

As for Old Medieval, it would be the centerpiece of Whirlee-Rels. The castle needed refurbishing, at a minimum, so it could double as a luxury hotel and convention center. It needed a swimming pool and a spa, at least two restaurants—a fancy one and a family one—a much bigger bar, maybe a casino. Bring in the big spenders. That's where the money was. The more high-end it got, the more everyone would scrimp and save so they could bring their brats for a vacation.

They even took a brief stroll into the forest. It could be turned into a great golf course. They picked up a pinch of soil and rubbed it between their fingers. Great for sand traps.

Syns objected to a few things, especially the ideas for the zoo. But overall they could see the merits of the parents' vision. Someone were bound to snap up H-town at some point. Times change.

After the tour they all went back to the Hornets' for a reprise of the day before. Such was the bonhomie that by the end of the day the parents were punching Syns on the rerebraces. "You got a good head under that helmet there, Dwarfie. We could see you in arbitrage, which is just a fancy word for good oriental rug dealing. We'll definitely find a place for you at Whirlee."

Sleep, eventually, collected them all.

Rels were still limiting visitors to their parents the following day. Syns were impatient to see them but even Tels were not allowed in.

Another breakfast with the parents in the ruin. Champagne sunrises and gimlets going up the straw. One parent were scarcely drinking.

"You feeling okay?" asked Syns.

"Tip-top. But we're taking off after breakfast and somebody's got to be the pilot. Listen, when you see Rels, let 'em know how important they're—see, we're learning—going to be in the new park. Get them to stop this idiotic sword-fighting. We need them unscarred for photoshoots. Speaking of cameras, we need to get the exact numbers on the books here. Investors are no dummies. You ever see one of these before?" A very small camera was displayed. "Go over to that city hall and take pictures. The last year should be good enough."

"Take pictures?"

"Yeah. Of the books, the account books."

"What do we tell people?"

231

"Zip. Go in at night when everybody's home watching reruns. And snap snap snap. Oh, and by the way, take off that armor for the job. Wear dark clothing."

Snap snap snap. Something in fact did snap—awake: Syns' conscience. "Well, hey. We don't know about breaking in."

"Dwarfie, what they don't know won't hurt 'em. First rule of good business. It's not like it's classified information. We just want to get the jump on the competition. Always get the jump. Second rule of good business. Don't get caught though. We'll never admit to any part of it. Third rule."

Syns wondered what it was about the castle that brought on such profoundly unpleasant surprises. "Sorry," they said, standing up and heading for the door, "we just remembered something." They ran.

Without word to anyone they saddled Whooshes and fled a second time.

Beyond the Last Resort

SYNS FLEW TO THE BACK GATE of M and through to the quiet of Arcady. Internally, however, all was noisy chaos. Whence this unsuspected darkness in our soul, this willingness to enter into a compact with the very devils? Capitalists. If they hadn't asked us to break the law, would we be there still, drinking and transmogrifying beyond all recognition?

We are so incredibly weak. The one thing we had managed to hold onto through all our disenchantments was our sense of values. But all it took was the possibility of aiding our quest for love and we jettisoned everything we'd ever believed in. Couldn't do it fast enough. The parents wanted us to agree to overthrowing the equal pay rule; it was *our idea*, probably the only good one we ever had. We do not recognize ourselves. We are even worse than we had thought, and that was pretty bad.

They felt so tired they could barely move. There was an aching weight in the chest area: disappointment in Rels. The buckshot of it. We had wanted to learn about the Sovereign. We did. The knowledge has killed our love. The splendor we attributed to Rels was the golden mote in our own eye. The fairy dust in the air was sprinkled by our own hand. Reality has arrived: the gold is turned to lead, the magic dust to prosaic dun. We have lost our lover's gift of alchemy.

You fall out of love due to some trait of the other. Then

you change, accept the trait, and fall into love again. The cycles go on for awhile—disillusionment, adaptation—until you reach a critical point and love snap like a rubber band finally stretched too far.

Beyond the last resort. The psyche work to maintain love as long as possible, utilizing frank psychosis as necessary. Bending reality, bending heaven and earth, until the last possible moment. And then, if pressured beyond endurance, it give up. The end come suddenly.

Who are we anyway? Rels are, in many ways, the enemy. What if they were a serial killer? Are there no limits to what we would overlook? And if we did manage to fall in love with them again, what could be the meaning of love for someone you hoped would fail at all their goals?

We are benumbed. Only emptiness, no succor anywhere. We made a new life in order to pursue Rels, in order to become worthy of their love. But we overlooked one critical thing—we made no provision for the complete unworthiness of both of us.

Our Work

NOWHERE TO TURN. The valley was ruined. They rode to their old campsite in Arcady, now empty of all supplies. They dismounted and lay down where their sleeping bag used to be.

They awoke feeling anxious. It was evening.

What should we do? We feel so alone. See a friend? What friend? Have we ever even had a friend? We had acquaintances but there were only one soul with whom we had crossed the divide of appearances.

You think some things that happen to you are not particularly significant, especially when they take place in the shadow of a grand dramatic event like the turn. But finding a friend is a rare thing, important unto necessity.

Plus, this friend were so odd, in ways so entirely different from ourselves, they made us feel just a little bit better about our own failings. Or not quite so bad. Lest we forget, we just sold our soul, almost.

Our hero stuffed cotton in their ears to protect themselves from the siren songs of suicide and rode to the copse.

The Hermit's door was open; a bit of light was meandering outside. Cautiously, Syns took out a piece of cotton. There was the sound of rasping exhalations. Shooh, shooh. They dismounted and moved closer. A pleasant, vaguely familiar chemical smell grew stronger.

"Hullo? Hermit?"

Shooh, shooh.

Syns peered inside. Someone were turning a hand-cranked ditto machine but it weren't the Hermit. Syns cleared their throat loudly. The stranger raised their head.

Taken by surprise, Syns' own head jerked backwards like a chicken. "Fols?"

The printer turned away. When they turned back, the familiar wild hair was upon them. "Knight, why are you here? We are busy."

Syns wrenched off their helmet. "Do you recognize us?"

"You are the Silver Dwarf Knight who came before."

"And who else? *Look* at us!"

"Jees, calm down."

"Syns! We are Syns!"

The printer looked at them closely. "Jees." There was a long pause. "You aren't writing about us are you?"

"We gave up writing. We hated it."

After another pause the Hermit tore off the wig. "We hate *this* thing."

The old friends embraced awkwardly.

"Even though it are you, we have to get back to work," said Fols.

"Can we help?"

Syns were soon cranking the ditto machine while Fols gathered, collated, and stapled pages together and stuffed them into envelopes.

Later Fols said, "You've earned a bit of a break. We can converse for a few minutes."

They went out and sat on their tree-roots by the creek.

236

"How are Glyphs?"

Fols sighed. "Relationships are never easy. Glyphs are inflexible and demanding but hopefully we will work it out. Are you still mooning over your love?"

Syns blurted out the whole story of their shameful lapse with the parents. "Can you believe it? We were willing to abandon all our values. We were completely insane."

Fols were thoughtful. Finally they said, "We have something to show you. Follow us."

They went back into the hut, to the second room where the rock appeared to be resting on their altar.

"Hello, Glyphs."

"They like you, you know. We're having dinner after we finish printing. You're invited."

"Thank you. We'll see."

Fols opened a door at the back of the room and carried the lantern into a third room, the largest. In its center a typewriter and a stack of pristine ditto masters sat on a high table. A cot was folded nearby.

Syns looked to the walls. They were covered with clipboards arranged in neat rows and columns, with papers clamped tightly in their jaws.

"Our work," said Fols. They took down a clipboard and scribbled a note on the top page. "This one is for Whirlee."

"Was my disgraceful confession of any help?"

"Definitely. Thanks."

"You will fight them?"

"We already are. And many others. Each clipboard is for a different threat to H-town. The work is endless. Many want to exploit it and some simply wish to eradicate it. Dangers come from inside too."

Syns flinched. Had things gone differently, there might be a clipboard just for themselves. "What about the poets' drill team?"

Fols went to another clipboard which gripped only a few pages. "For now we are watching. We don't know what, if any, threat they pose. But we have good news too." They swept a hand to another wall of clipboards. "Others around the world are interested in our polity and wish to emulate it. The scope of the work expands."

As Syns listened a boulder lifted from their chest. Fols, the person they had most admired. Not an exemplar in matters of love, but in terms of values no one had stayed more true.

Syns experimentally thought of Rels. Did any vestige of love remain? Perhaps. Probably. Yes.

". . . revolution, one way or another . . ."

Syns remembered those meetings long ago and Fols' stirring words. We wanted above all else to be like them and become a revolutionary. Having no idea what that meant except that it would be glorious. And now? Whatever it were, it were not glorious.

". . . no neutral ground. If you are not a revolutionary you are contributing to reactionary thought . . ."

It would be challenging to be with Rels, to be with a

reactionary lover. But not impossible. We must continue to be ourselves, somehow.

". . . equality of power, of agency, of money, of freedom . . ."

Rels' parents would object to our love. Too bad for them. These are not medieval times. As for our parents, they would object for the opposite reasons. Too bad for them too.

". . . falseness about H-town. It is far from self-sufficient. Though it is more or less egalitarian, it feeds off the capitalist world around it and panders to it. A vest pocket utopia is no longer enough. We must have a revolution of intention and means and . . ."

Sometimes we doubt the morality of our being in love at all. We will have to become much stronger. Learn to argue, to hold our position.

". . . the argument is with capitalism but . . ."

Good old Fols. Still accelerating into oratory.

". . . industrialism, overpopulation, the resources of the planet . . ."

So reassuring, such consistency. "Are you trying to woo us back to the cause?" asked Syns with a smile.

"You are in the throes of love so we are not trying very hard." Fols sighed. "We talked about our own love last time you were here. We feel guilty: we cannot be as pure as our ideals. The truth are we barely manage. Perhaps if you had a rock—we might be able to fix you up. Speaking of which, have you decided about dinner? We have to finish up with the dittoing."

Syns were clear. "We need to get home now. May we visit again?"

"Only if you are ready to work."

"What could we do?"

"Everything."

Moonlight Ride

OUR KNIGHT SET OUT on their trusty steed. It was a beautiful warm night. The full moon was in the sky, huge and ivory. Leaves were sparkling black.

They splashed across the causeway. Where the algae was disturbed, the swamp glistened like a pool of oil. They felt cured by the visit with Fols. They had work to do, a tournament to prepare for.

Despite their new knowledge of themselves—their vulnerability to the softening of their values over the bunsen burner of love—it was a beautiful night and they were happy.

And Rels? They are entirely other. What they do are out of our control.

They had surrendered. They were in love and that were the end of it. So many times they had thought love were over. It always returned, more certain than before, in greater reality and truth.

And what if they never won them? What if they were one of so many who loved from afar for a lifetime? If it were thus, they asked but one thing: that their love be known. The next time they saw Rels they would tell them.

If some new information were ever to end our love we would not go back to our old life. We would remain on our quest for extraordinary ordinary love. For it are better to be in love than not.

The grain of sand provokes the oyster to the pearl. In

this way doth love provoke us to coat its irritations with layers of meaning and of beauty.

Things that have become loved because they have some relationship to the beloved: moon, air, gravity, surface of the earth—in short, everything.

Syns felt, for a moment, calmly, that they would be good for Rels.

Whooshes leapt up the escarpment, then wove down into the valley; all the while the moon shone clear and bright.

Arriving at their valley home Syns shed their armor. They fed and groomed Whooshes, then themselves. They climbed the ladder and branches to the tree-house. They lay down and looked up at the kindly lunar face, close enough for a whispered conversation.

Termites

DID THEY HEAR SOMETHING IN THE BRANCHES going che che che?

A fallen log at the edge of a meadow.

Within, oppressed nation of termites. Workers on an assembly line, unhappy, sighing. Owners lounge in comfort. Managers goad the workers, "More, more."

Dissidents paint surrealist pictures, perform street theater in channels of wood. Firebrands orate at secret meetings, plotting.

The workers turn on the managers and owners. No more labor unless changes are made. They leave the log, have a party in the meadow. Dancing, flirting, falling in love easily.

Night falls. Full moon with termite face. Laughter in the summer warmth.

Work to be done the next day. Managers and owners are gone, now they are workers too. All side by side, doing as little as is needed.

Maximum freedom, maximum equality, maximum justice. They sing as they work.

Happy termite nation now.

Preparation

SYNS AWOKE FEELING RESTED, EAGER to begin. The Harvest Festival was seven days away.

They scrambled down to Whooshes. They all breakfasted in the meadow.

Syns fashioned a set of rings and a smooth-spinning quintain. Knight and horse spent a couple of hours in light training. They stopped for grooming, lunch, and a nap. In the afternoon they had another training session. The valley was quiet except for the woodpeckerish sound of lance-strike on target.

They foraged widely. Sweet acorn, nut, grape, berry, wild crab apple.

Evening dinner and early to bed.

Knowing that the tournament was not for winning love but for demonstrating it.

In love and sane at last.

Book Four: The First of October

The Seventh Morning

THE SEVENTH MORNING, the first of October. Syns were excited, nervous. They dressed in shining armor and mounted their splendidly groomed and barded horse.

Of course they might lose the joust against Cyras. The important thing was to comport themselves well. Execute to the best of their ability what they had been practicing. They felt healthy, prepared.

Would they find love? They could not imagine it. Perhaps they were not meant for such strong things. It were best to love without expectation. Their goal was to declare their love. Additionally, though unlikely, to receive a favor.

What if they were injured? Then so be it. Even if they were to die—hardly imaginable, but still—they had lived a wonderful life, for it had led to this exquisite morning.

Though nervous they were also calm. They would show up and give their utmost. More than that could not be asked.

Now There Have Come One

THE SKY WAS A FRESH CLEAR BLUE with the golden thread of fall.

Our silver-clad knight crossed the causeway. In Arcady Forest birds orated, the creek giggled. The first sound of Harvest Festival aroused the air: herald of horns. As they neared they heard singing, fiddles, laughing, a general throbbing hum. They entered the back gate of M. Ahead, banners flew high.

They saw Hercs, Friths, Els, and several other muckers on their way, undoubtedly, to the ale tent before proceeding to work in the lists. As Syns rode up beside them Hercs called out, "Silver Dwarf! you made it!"

"We wagered you would. All of us except Friths here," said Els.

"Well," said Friths, "we were thinkin' as might be a fool's job, goin' up 'gainst the giant. Thought yer might be wiser not ter show."

"But most of us think foolhardiness is your specialty," laughed Hercs. "And here you are, riding in out of nowhere, another of your traits. Then you'll disappear again, eh?"

Syns were pleased to see their old friends. On impulse they said, "You know us well, don't you?"

"How can we? You're the knight who never trains. At least not here," said Hercs.

"We did once. You trained us!"

The muckers laughed heartily at this.

"Don't you remember Akas?"

"Akas! That crazy mucker disappeared on us."

"And?"

"And what?"

"Think back."

"They were always talking about how they were going to become a knight. And Whooshes disappeared the same night. Maybe Akas stole them, we've often thought."

"And who are this fine horse if they aren't Whooshes?"

Hercs looked hard at the horse. Syns could sense the moment they recognized the armor and the horse beneath. "So they are. Did you buy them from that thief Akas, then?"

"Think, friends. Friths, surely you remember that night you were out smoking in the field and we were there and you told us of the job."

"Blow us over with a horse fart! 'Tis yerselves!" shouted Friths.

"Now wish us luck you stinky louts."

"And to think we were the one who introduced you to Whooshes. Well, Akas, you have good taste in your thievery. Come to the ale tent with us, all the same," said Hercs, shaking their head.

"We can't."

"Yer really goin' through with it then?" asked Friths.

"Why not? We were trained by the best, weren't we?"

"For your sake, we hope so," said Hercs. "Stop by

and see us if you don't get yourself killed."

"Aye." With a wave Syns passed on.

"Silvers!" Rins of the fan club.

"Hey Rins! Hail!"

"Did you hear the news? The Sovereign are coming down from the tower. Television people are here, biggest crowd ever. Guess you know you have a lot of fans now, too."

"Last we heard it was nine."

"Where have you been? You're colossal. Second only to Rels."

But Syns were not prepared for the shouts that went up when they passed the cathedral and were amidst the multitude.

"Now there have come one who will take the measure!"

"Measure a bit short though, don't they?"

"So sexy."

Syns had never overheard a compliment behind their back before. They felt a momentary thrill. What a beautiful day. In love, loving everyone.

"Silver Dwarf! Silver Dwarf!"

The hysterical edge in the voice was unmistakable. Blats the fan, a paper-mâché falcon on their shoulder, were tugging on Syns' saboton.

"We do not love you and we never will!" Syns could not restrain themselves from shouting.

"You already told us that. How about an autograph."

Syns were so relieved they gladly signed the program

Blats held up: Good luck and best regards, the Silver Dwarf Knight.

Blats read it. "Oh," they said, somewhat crestfallen. Suddenly they brightened."Thank you, we love you!"

At the edge of the throng in shroudish white stood Jults. They gazed ahead blankly. Syns made their way over to them. "We have news about Fols."

Jults bent over, shrieking.

Panic zipped through Syns. "Sorry, sorry."

Jults straightened, howling with laughter. "You should be ashamed of yourselves! Nothing can separate us. Certainly not you!"

"Sorry."

Further on they saw Frits, ex-agent, walking along with Gots, ex-publisher. Both were dressed in the cloaks for sale at the gate. With them were Gans, cheesemaker and literary novelist. The three were engrossed in conversation. Syns called out a greeting. They raise their heads, looked around, then resumed talking to each other.

A familiar wild head of hair in the crowd. Syns rode up beside it. "So there *are* some things that will take you away from your work."

"They forced us to bring them. They are cheering for you." Fols rolled their eyes and pointed to an embroidered pouch around their neck.

Syns laughed as they rode on.

The duo-jester Livs and Lucs were in the long line at the ale tent waving their tankards.

"The Silver Dwarf are here!" said Livs.

"We don't see anything," said Lucs.

"Do ye see *us*?"

"Wherefore art this irritating voice coming from?" Lucs were peering at the merry crowd.

Also in line were the barkeeps Stils and Gils, Duns from the mailroom, and familiar faces from the Butts: Rofs the dance troupe director as a troubadour with a tambourine, Wims the plumber-acrobat, Kyrs the shepherd, and Trops the wheelwright.

Booths lined the entrance to the tournament field. Syns recognized Fars peddling weavings; Flys, candles; and Pors, little cakes.

All along the way there were shouts of "Silver Dwarf!" "Good luck!" "We love you!"

A piercing wail. Syns looked over. The weeper Skrimps were sitting on a hay bale, clutching a bare foot, rocking back and forth. Syns waved but tarried not.

Finally they reached the lists. Syns had dismounted and were signing in when Ayrds ran over in gleaming armor that appeared to be trimmed in gold. They were grinning. "Silvers! Wow! You made it! Some tourney!"

"Sure is."

"Did you hear the news? National television! Isn't that great? Did you know you're famous?"

"We?"

"Yeah, verily, Some people keep coming by asking if you've gotten here yet. There they are again!" Ayrds pointed at Syns, shouting, "Over here!"

Someone holding a microphone sidled close to Syns, while someone holding a camera shoved people aside.

"We're with the Silver Dwarf Knight, who will be going up against the Giant Cyras in the opening joust this afternoon." The interviewer seemed to be trying to crawl inside Syns' armor, grinning as if they were old friends. "Tell the viewers, how are you feeling about your chances?"

"Uh, pretty good."

"The question everyone're asking is 'Where have you been hiding?'"

"That's a secret, actually."

"Mysterious! Like the fact that you never take off your helmet or raise up your visor?"

"Yeh."

"Do you have any special words for the special audience here today?"

What were they talking about? Were Rels here? "Well, uh . . ."

"Take a look over at that roped-off area. Those kids in wheelchairs are all winners of the Whirlee essay contest. They had to write about why they wanted to be here today. A lot of them wrote about you, how you're an inspiration because you don't let being a dwarf stop you from going after what you want. Wonderful, huh?"

"Uh. Yeh."

"And here you are, about to square off against someone twice your size."

"Um—"

A roaring cheer from the stands.

Syns looked over. Rels had just entered from the castle's postern gate, surrounded by their retinue. Syns' heart leapt like a flushed rabbit. When they turned back, the interviewer and camera-person were running toward the Sovereign, tripping over their robes.

"Great, huh?" Ayrds were still there. "It's our first tournament. We're up right after you and Cyras, with the juniors. By the way, we're supposed to give the special kids a salute during the promenade."

"Okay. Hey, good luck."

"You too."

While a small band played, the parade of animals were winding their way around the tournament grounds. The entire F-town zoo were there, some animals tame enough to walk freely, some on tethers, others, too dangerous, in cages in ox-drawn wooden carts.

The stands were filling rapidly.

The Mayor of Old M, holding the ceremonial mallet and block of wood, were finding their seat in the section directly in front of the awning for the nobility. Beside the Mayor were the Sheriff, with a large wooden whistle hung around their neck, and the Keepers of Order, with truncheons and smaller whistles.

Rels left the reporters and ascended toward the tournament throne.

Out of Turn

WHOOSHES WERE BEHAVING like a veteran. Excited yet calm, strong, beautiful, completely attuned to their rider.

"We stole well, buddies," said Syns. They took their place in line just behind Cyras, followed by the rest of the knights. They all filed forth and trotted around the field. People threw flowers, shouted, and cheered. Syns nodded to the special kids, who yelled and rocked their wheelchairs back and forth.

After the promenade lap the audience sat down, all except for Rels, who held a square of gold silk trimmed in purple. The giant cantered out on Phantoms.

Syns' body were trembling. This is it, the final exam. What a beautiful day to die, of humiliation or otherwise. They urged Whooshes forward and passed Cyras.

Rels frowned slightly and said, "Silver Dwarf Knight, it is not your turn yet. Ye are next, for Tels."

The crowd hooted and cheered in good-natured derision. Syns did not move, wondering if they were going to have a heart attack.

When the hooting died down they said in a loud voice, "We fight for you, Sovereign, whether you will have it or no." They were absolutely clear, worthy and unashamed.

A great prize was already won: the reclamation of the selves. With this came a dizzying return, wrenching as travel through time, to innocence, to the open heart of childhood.

As for the prize of love—without the transformation you could never keep it. Yes, we are the same person. The same eyes look out upon the world, the same mind think, the same body act. Syns felt compassion for their younger selves, so full of vague ambition. We were a better person than we knew. We were, in a way, indomitable. Even unto this day we have not given up our dreams, not even of love. So magnificent is the world. We love our life, which are hardly a fairy tale. A real human life. We could ask for nothing better.

Cyras had come up next to Syns. The crowd were murmuring, thrilled.

Rels were still for a moment. They looked over at Tels, who smiled and inclined their head. Then the Sovereign carefully tore the golden square in two. They tied a piece to the end of each presented lance: Cyras' first, Syns' second. Our hero tried not to think that the order of the bestowing held any significance.

A thundering cheer went up.

"Ye shallen regret this, fool midget," said the giant through clenched teeth.

But Syns knew this was the first act of their life that was entirely without regret, whatever the consequences.

They rode to their respective ends of the tilt. Syns removed their favor and placed it next to their heart. They glanced over at Cyras.

The giant had dropped their lance. Their clumsy squire were fumbling around in the dirt and strewn hay.

Syns patted the noble Whooshes. "Hah! They don't look so confident now." They had accomplished both their goals—declared for Rels and received a favor.

Now they had a new goal: to fight and win.

This Moment

A TRUMPET SOUNDED four sharp blasts, *dum dah dah DAH!* All eyes turned toward the combatants. Some knights remained mounted, some stood beside their horses.

The giant lowered their visor. Syns', of course, was already in place. Lances went into rests. Whooshes snorted, eager for the fray.

Cyras were a mountain of black steel. It were inconceivable that this goliath could lose.

"Allez allez allez." The signal hand came down.

The two knights galloped toward each other.

The shaft of Cyras' lance dipped and accidentally touched Phantoms' shaffron. The sound of metal on metal rang and clanged and banged. Syns felt a pang of fear. This was not the lance that had been presented to the Sovereign.

The Mayor were standing, pounding their board with the mallet, shouting, "Desist in the name of the Crown!" The whistle of the Sheriff shrilled.

Neither knight slowed in their rush toward destiny.

Syns saw the metal lance, painted to look like wood, sharpened to a point.

We may die here today. So be it. This is the pinnacle of all we have ever been, all we have ever aspired to be. Without reason, even without meaning, simply to be in this sunshine, in complete reality and clarity. In which all sensation is perfect, in the perfection of life itself. Knowing surrender, knowing courage, which is action without the necessity of hope.

The crowd were shouting. Rels were standing, the Sheriff and Keepers were on the field.

Certainty, terror, determination, adrenaline. Calm. This moment.

Passion and Disorder

WHOOSHES WERE REARING UP, impossibly high, jumping backwards at the same time, like flying. They shrieked and shuddered and Syns flew into the air.

Time slowed. Syns knew their magnificent horse had sacrificed themselves.

The vectors of motion brought Syns down on the horse's back. Saddle, bridle, barding, and coverings, were gone. Syns clutched at the mane. "Whoa, buddies, whoa."

But horse no longer responded to human. They ran around the field, bellowing. The other horses, seized with empathic wildness, sprang forth and careened through the grounds, some without riders, some with helpless ones.

The zoo animals joined the fray. H-buffalo stampeded across the field, joined by zebras, giraffes and donkeys. Pigs squealed behind. Augustuss, overcome with emotion, scrambled away from their tender. Parrots and peacocks flew up, crying. Oxen broke free from their carts. Two bears battered down the wooden bars of their cage and lumbered out.

Syns watched: in the midst of action and an observer outside it.

The crowd screamed as the animals turned toward the stands. A bear scrambled toward a thickly spectacled child in a wheelchair. Pieces of metal flew upward.

The pitch of screams went higher. Spectators were

pushing, falling down, trampling each other, while rising up toward them were the mass of animals like beasts from hells.

Through the main gate raced a police-car, ambulance, and fire engine, sirens at full volume.

Whooshes leapt into the stands and headed straight at Rels. Syns held on, pulling back on the mane as if to tear it out by the roots. The horse gave a mighty shake and Syns were falling, slowly, wondering if they would be crushed under the hooves of the horses behind them.

They had but one wish—that Rels be spared.

Unblink of an Eye

THEY WERE ON THEIR SIDE, bouncing mercilessly.

They opened their eyes. A horse's neck was in their line of vision. Tree trunks and branches were flying past.

"Whooshes?"

"Don't try to sit up."

The Ragged Band

HISSING, MUMBLING, MOANING. Syns opened their eyes. They were lying on the marshy ground by the swamp. They sat up quickly.

Rels were nearby with Whooshes. Strips of the royal robe had been tied together and around the horse.

"Sovereign?"

"Your poor horse tried to run into the swamp. It were all we could do to stop them. Easy there. Easy there." They patted Whooshes.

Syns came over and patted the horse too.

"They saved your life," said Rels.

"Apparently so did you. How bad is the injury?"

"Fortunately their initial jump prevented the lance from going in too deep. But the wound is in a very sensitive area."

Syns winced. They embraced the horse's head. "Buddies."

"*Hsss*—ty-seven injured, thirteen in critical condition, four of them children. Some have been helicoptered out to neighboring hos—*hsss* . . ." The sounds were coming from somewhere in the royal garments.

"We suppose you must go back now," said Syns, unable to hold back a sigh.

"Not just yet."

"Would you . . . there's a causeway we built across the swamp. We would like to take you to—across it."

"*Hsss*—ras, currently being held without—*hsss* . . ."

"Okay, let's go," said Rels.

"Go ahead, buddies."

Whooshes stepped confidently onto the invisible causeway. Syns went next, saying, "Watch exactly where we step." Rels were last.

"*Hsss*—cariest thing we ever saw! Unbelievable! We thought for sure the stands were going to col—*hsss* . . ."

The ragged band continued, strolling of an afternoon, all on a carpet of green.

The First Humans

WHOOSHES STEPPED ONTO THE ROCK. Syns climbed over on hands and knees. They turned to assist Rels but the Sovereign had already jumped across. They walked to the top of the escarpment and looked down into the valley below.

"Are we enchanted?" Rels finally asked.

"Perhaps. This is where we have been staying, where we trained."

Whooshes pawed at the stone, eager to continue.

"The wound needs to be bathed again," said Rels.

"There's a creek in the valley. Follow us."

Whooshes led the way into the shadow of the valley. They went directly to the creek and lay down. They shrieked once and were quiet.

Rels threw off their robes and went toward the water.

Should we look at them? wondered Syns. The circumstances are so peculiar. A knight would not look unless invited. They averted their eyes.

Rels splashed cheerfully. "This feels so good. Take off your armor and join us."

In a moment of forgetfulness, Syns glanced over. All that covered the Sovereign was a small radio on a strap around their neck. Struck blind by lust. If they reject us now we would never recover. Just put us in a padded room next to Jults. They looked quickly away.

Rels laughed.

265

What shall we do? Courage ever demand more courage. They took off all their coverings—including, with some trepidation, their helmet—and stepped into clear cool water.

Later Syns and Rels dried Whooshes and replaced the bandage. At one point Syns slipped and bumped against the Sovereign. They fell together into the long grass. Syns could not suppress a groan of agony. Here were Rels beneath them, unclothed. They rolled aside and sat up. "Sorry."

They fed and groomed the horse and settled them in their shelter.

"I would like to show you my home."

Syns climbed the ladder first. In the branches they reached down and lent their hand to Rels. Every time they touched, Syns thought they would fall or float away. They were burning up, freezing. Surely we are the first humans, at the beginning of civilization.

Higher and higher they climbed. The wide sea appeared, calm as a blessing, turning to lavender-gray in the evening light.

Bunked and Debunked

A LIGHT BREEZE. They move the tarp aside and uncover the sleeping bags. They zip them together. Rels slide in. Syns follow.

Syns are trying to believe that they are existing in a real world. So much important information suddenly so near at hand. The lover no longer afar. Aclose. *Would* they be lovers?

It are one thing to declare one's love in front of everyone and then face death. Simple actions.

But to reach out now.

They extend a hand, touch Rels on the shoulder. Birds fly within. The turbulence causes them to bend forward.

"Silver Dwarf Knight. Yet more bravery."

They roll over and cover the length—almost the length— of Rels' body.

Heart beating so hard it must surely be dangerous. Breathing in small bursts, the lungs having forgotten their routine function. The mind alternately blank and racing. The old unworthiness. A lifetime of happiness. The in different cosmos. Dread of the sudden awakening. And, and, and, Rels.

Forming words a task too complicated. Our lips brush against the neck of the other. Who moan—and their hand reaches out and takes our own hand, brings it to their lips.

Slow. Annihilation.

It are already enough. The mind cannot fathom any-thing more. But the body do not care. Prayers from an-cient times when all the world was holy. Move. Sense. Stop. Pay attention. Move again.

Kiss. Saliva of the other. A new universe cohabited. Part of us now. This whole new body grown so suddenly upon our own. If the other move, we move. If the other blink, we blink. This second body have but one failing: we cannot feel sensations as strongly as with our first body. Yet our awareness of the second body are more acute. Breath. A connection between movement of the chest and stream of air through the nostrils. A connection be-tween beating heart and pulse at the wrist. Stomach gurgles. Throat swallows. Muscle twitches. Lock of hair caught up in a gravitational wave, falls.

Music. Atonal, cacophonous. The conductor, bewil-dered, step down from the podium; the mad musicians of the body play on. Each try to be loudest. But the high trebles, the deep basses, are winning. They rise above, bur-row below the others. The rest of the orchestra lose in-terest and wander off, their sounds grow distant. While the lunatic flutes, the anarchic tympani, play even louder, until there are no other sounds in the universe.

Until teeth swell, nails liquefy, hair throbs, mitochon-dria quiver, sodium channels flood, livers sigh, skulls col-lapse, blood melts, skin have a nervous breakdown, toes take flight, lymph nodes moan, and hearts spin and spin and spin until—centrifugal force wins out. Fragments of heart rain down for miles.

What is the most important thing about sex? The most important thing is that it are not the most important thing. Sex are not what command you. Sex are a squall, a tornado in the midst of a grander storm. Sex are a narrative with a comprehensible plot in the middle of a greater epic whose conclusions are unknown. Sex are frail compared to love.

Love are something you carry in your chest like pounds of lead every day. Worry, joy, exasperation, vulnerability. Powerful as a fatal disease.

And somehow, ignorant fool that we are, we manage to know this: in sex and in love, the degree of pleasure or otherwise are primarily one's own predilection.

Rels were already in the quiet breath of sleep. Syns joined them.

It was night when Syns woke up. Under the half-moon they stole down to check on Whooshes. By lanternlight they inspected the wound. No further bleeding.

Whooshes stirred. Knight and horse crossed the meadow to the creek. Syns washed them, dried them, fed them oats. Spoke to them awhile. Settled them again.

They climbed back up to the treehouse and lay beside Rels, skin to skin.

Thinking

WE ARE DEFINITELY IN LOVE. Are Rels in love also? What did this day mean to them? No words have been spoken. We are crushed in a vise of hope. Rels are naked beside us. We are calmer and happier than usual.

The fan club, the photos we memorized. Fuel of our folly, now made real. And other galvanisms—during the pursuit, at the conquest, immediately afterwards.

Sex are pleasurable. Must it be more than that? Must we argue about a glass of wine, a sunset? We must. For the attempted unification of sex and love we must converse, and conversation is fundamentally an argument.

Let us suppose that you have a terrible time believing that you are loved but the fact is that you are. Then you will have to imagine the possibility until such time as you can know its truth. Sometimes, if you are managing to let love in a bit, the task are so difficult it's not a good time for sex. Better to have a normal conversation. Slow down.

In some ways guilt are vanity. If you are humble enough you know it are not even you who are having success. Guilt are humility gone bad.

What giddy things are hermaphrodites! The deep wild pain of passionate love. The need to survive it, often just barely.

The beauty of experience increases libido. Love increase the experience of beauty. Such dangerous synergy.

The power that the beauty of the world has over

us. We need a vessel to contain it. In the maelstrom wrought by beauty, we wayward barnacles need something to fasten onto: for us it are Rels.

We watch for the dilation of pupil, the twitch of muscle; we listen to the tension of the vocal cords, the depth of breath. Ultimately we cannot lie to each other. In the crucible of love, falseness is burned away, eventually.

What are the realities of the person we love and what do they matter? We want Rels forever, for all of it—sex, the day to day, problems, everything. Actual love for another person, not a metaphor for death or selves-involvement.

We begin to think we have something to offer: we shall love them but we shall not become them. We possess an independent mind. Also, our knowledge. Even though Rels are dazzlingly charismatic, loved by all, they have defects. We will try to be satisfied with them as they are, and not mistake them for—or attempt to make them into— our perfect other. Resist sailing toward that shoal of in-evitable shipwreck.

Loving from above. Always we have made ourselves lower. However low the other were, we flattened ourselves in order to be even lower. With effort we shall barely be from above. Only a millimeter but it are enough.

Rels need us to love them from above. Or, to put it another way, they need for us to allow them to love us from below. They need our anarchistic love. To be a suc-cessful lover of the charismatic other, you must allow them to look up to you. The charismatic person are the one likely to do the emulating and you must allow it in good grace. There are the bond with the other, and there are also the bond, in the sense of vow, to the world, to the others who love them also.

There were a charismatic person, an artist, who found love with a professor of mathematics who were not charismatic at all. What attracted the artist were the professor's superiority. The reverse were not the case: the artist were not ideal for the mathematician but they tolerated the situation quite well because they were so independent. The mathematician filtered everything through their own eyes, steadfast in their analysis of the world. They included the artist in their life, took them seriously like one of their equations, albeit an unsolvable one.

In the past we were a supplicant. We were in error. We did not distinguish between charisma and superiority, did not know to make the topological point ourselves, the pre-Copernican construction. The charismatic other already have too much adoration, too many who bow down. That are the last thing they need from us.

A writer once said that persons who love more are inferior and must suffer. They were wrong. Superior and inferior are like anatomical descriptors—the superior mesenteric artery, the inferior vena cava. They have nothing to do with who love more; rather, they refer to who are more able to shelter the other in their independence.

We seem to have a tiny bit of charisma too, which we have never understood. Fortunately, it are irrelevant.

Romance of Romance

What would happen to us if love were attained? We would try to go on. We have learned the value of hard work, of surrender. Love are about these things. Writing ceased to be hard work except in terms of enduring its distastefulness. It became too easy; that was part of what made it so hateful. We now know we are capable of sustained intense effort. We may grumble a bit but in fact we are relieved.

The truth are, love solve nothing except love. And that are at its best, often it cannot even solve itselves. Good or bad, love must simply be added on to everything else. Like taking up boxing as a hobby and coming home beat up from the gym every night. Adding that to one's already overwhelming life, eyes swollen almost shut, lips fat and cut, bruised everywhere, exhausted. It do not matter; one must still feed the livestock, make dinner, do all the other tasks of life. Love are no excuse.

Can you have romantic love if you are under siege from starvation, war, slavery? Are it only a blandishment for the privileged? Certainly if it are unrequited one feel less guilty for one's situation, and kinship with others who suffer. But success? Who have that? Can one in good conscience want that too? Who could be honorable while possessing such good fortune?

Vows and images from childhood. Were they of any value? Beautiful, profound, but one were a child and did not know the world: the vast swaths of suffering over which beauty dropped its veil. All we knew was that life seemed so much more ecstatic to us than to our parents.

The very first thing we wanted to be, even before CSH at age four, were an artist. Because of beauty; it conquered us so thoroughly. What could we do except become its servant?

Mythos of creativity. Luring romantic youth into becoming painters, poets, composers. But also choreographers of genocide, architects of war. You can be moved unto undying passion and do horrific things. When the romantic impulse breaks the leash to the lover and the family and runs amok in the world, can there be any assurance that good will come of it?

Once we admired Fols, the only hero we ever had, and wanted to be a revolutionary. Our imagination and sense of morality were thrilled by their way of speaking and their vision for H-town. But what if the orator had not been Fols, but someone with a sinister agenda?

H-town. It is threatened, it could be destroyed. What if it came down to armed resistance? Where do you draw the line? For seeming eternity the questions are theoretical. Suddenly they become urgent.

Fols were once so appealing. Now—the wig, the rock. As for ourselves, we would prefer to be a hermit, we are so anxious and introverted.

Leaders are needed who can inspire both builders and fighters. Leaders who are fearless, who even enjoy some degree of danger.

Thinking Plus Talking

RELS STIRRED BESIDE THEM. "Mmmmm?"

Syns leaned over, kissed the beloved neck. The faintest pre-dawn light began to fill the sky.

"So we weren't dreaming," said the Sovereign.

"Both."

"And what are you doing, Silver Dwarf Knight?"

"Thinking."

"About what, my knight?"

"About armed resistance. Who should lead it."

Rels laughed. "You waste no time."

"We waste vast amounts of time, almost a lifetime. But not quite."

"We should go see Whooshes."

"We already did. Took them to the stream for a wash. The bleeding has stopped. They are sleeping."

Rels sat up and kissed Syns on the check. "You are a good knight."

"Not . . ." Accept the compliment. "Thank you." Thus it begins, the practice of loving from above.

Rels turned on the radio. "*Hsss*—is on for Rels the Sovereign and the mysterious Sil—"

Syns reached over and turned it off. "We must talk now. We must tell each other everything, hold nothing back."

There was a very long pause. Then Rels said, "There are someone else."

"We know." Devastation. So easily hidden. Simply

freeze. Better yet, just roll off the platform.

"No, not Cyras. Someone else."

"Another. That you love." A heart no longer wishing to beat.

"We think so. But we have little hope of it."

"Who could refuse you?"

"Oh, you know. Someone of greater intelligence. Greater courage. There must be no more risking your life like you did at the tournament."

Do they mean us? Was it a sequitur or non? A vitally important piece of information. "We refuse." Stalling for time.

"Why?"

"For selves-respect."

"You would disobey us. We are affronted."

"Don't be, for without it we cannot truly love." Time then, once and for all, for the ultimate act of courage. "And do you love us, Sovereign?"

"Silver Dwarf Knight, we do."

Everything that had ever fallen over was stood up, everything lost was found, everything sundered made whole.

A gigantic lump appeared in the throat, sudden as a volcanic island. "How did this happen?" A voice become a croak.

"Because of your actions and your honesty. Dishonesty are such cowardice."

Happiness are so odd. Who need it? There's not

enough room in the lungs for it. Like swallowing a helium balloon—difficult to take a breath, too much floating. How can you know how you feel unless you feel bad?

Then shall it be you and we who stay together for this lifetime? O gods, if not now. The eyes looking at us, mouth smiling. The face so close it is fractured, cubist. Even subtracting the sexual, hypothetically, the experience of something so intense: another, nothing stopping.

Everything have been for the best. Being loved by the one you wish would love you. Such a miracle it is unreasonable. Unfair to so many who live their days without it. Having in one's possession something so rare—stupendous as one of the seven wonders of the world—it should be part of the public domain.

Undoing: its myriad paths. Its widest road, the one most heavily trod, is surfeit. Thus the too-blessed lovers make it possible to endure themselves. Finding faults, growing accustomed and weary. By means of undoing we may tolerate our windfall.

If you stumble upon a treasure chest full of gold and jewels and are not allowed to give any of it away—but that is the answer: give it away. Except for the tornado of sex. Fides. Other than that, everything must be shared. The riches of love.

What about before, when our love were unrequited? Were simply loving not also a gift? At the time we were suffering too much to notice. But in retrospect, yes, that were a gift too. We already had more than we deserved.

Desire aside, the rest of the story of love are unknown. Rejoice in desire, then. Rejoice in what portion you know of love, requited or not. Suffer if you must but not too much. Not as much as we wallowed in. On the other hand, suffering were our education. We would know nothing had we not been enrolled. For us, for the romantics, it would appear to be our only path to understanding.

Who are these romantics? You cannot tell by looking, or even by knowing someone well, for it are often the one secret that is kept. That mathematician, that logician, that boxer, that garbage-collector, that prison guard, that criminal, that banker, and especially that cynic—might just be a romantic. Who then are not? It are also not known. The veil is drawn, either way. Some say the romantics are rare, some say they are common. Can one change from one to the other?

Rels were speaking ". . . don't understand it but we've learned that our body have an effect on people. Sometimes it doesn't seem that our body are even ours. It is as if it had been taken away from us, made into something public. Once it weren't a problem. It were just our body with its pleasures and pains. Now we sometimes wonder, What *are* this flesh?"

"But it happened to us, too. The adoration of you. It was at the High Summer Tournament. You were arguing with Cyras and you turned and . . . we were changed. Forever."

"The Summer Tournament. Hmmm." Rels thought

for a moment. "Oh, we remember. Cyras had—"

"Please. Don't explain."

"But you said we should tell each other everything, hold nothing back."

"Everything except that."

Rels smiled. "You are fortunate we do not require consistency."

"We are an H."

"And so are we." A pause. "There are so many who think they are in love with us. It seem horrible at times, to actually hurt people by not choosing them." Another pause. "Are that why you were so upset when we brought the fan to the castle?"

The fan. "Yes. To be precise, because the fan were exactly like ourselves with you."

"It were unfeeling of us, arrogant. We should have understood."

"You understand now. That is all we ask."

"There are something about you that amaze us."

Syns thought, This is one of those moments. To be from above. Rels need to look up to us. So utterly foreign. "And what are that?"

"A combination of great courage and also great humility. As if you do not know your gifts at all."

Hold hold hold. "Thank you."

Rels smiled. "We feel a bit inferior to you."

Hold. "What? How are that possible! We are nothing but a . . . thank you."

"We have developed a facade. No one know they have the power to hurt our feelings."

Syns learned something in that moment: the most terrifying thing in the world are letting ourselves be loved. We do not know the implications—what obligation, what guilt, what oppression may follow. We feel it coming toward us, growing larger like an oncoming train. How can we stand on the tracks and not run away in justified horror? "Perhaps we are similar." They remembered their chief criticism of Rels: their indifference to those who loved them. "We oscillate in and out of love. But we always come back to it, and stronger."

"We oscillate too."

"Do you come back stronger?"

"So far, no. But we would like to learn how it are done."

It were all too much. The tourney, the brush with death, being with Rels now. Syns looked at the Sovereign, who seemed much less perturbed. They were different. Danger did not bother them so much. They *chose* to fight from a rigging above a tower. We feel rather stunned and brutalized. If we cannot entirely feel our good fortune, at least we can recognize it. Somewhere we are happy. A faint echo of happiness reverberates from an unknown location within us. Yes, we should be happier but this are the best we can do. "One thing we will have to figure out are what to do about surfeit."

Rels laughed hard. "Already! Such a romantic!"

"What usually brings love back for us is the threat of

loss. How do anyone maintain love without having to resort to it?"

"What's wrong with the threat of loss?"

"It's too exhausting. We survived it, just barely, on our quest. But it is too much for daily life. There has to be another way."

"Perhaps one simply have to tolerate feelings of surfeit and wait for passion to return."

"Tolerate it while maintaining fidelity."

"Are that what you want?"

"Absolutely."

"We are no expert in fidelity. But we are not opposed." Rels paused. "Do you ever feel too privileged? Almost proud, and then ashamed of the pride?"

"We feel too privileged, or at least too lucky, when something good happens to us. As for pride, perhaps not." Syns thought awhile. "Tell us, you see us without our helmet."

"Without anything, our knight."

"Yes. Um, but do you recognize who we are?"

"You mean you are not the Silver Dwarf Knight from a small country far away?"

"No."

"Who are you then?"

"We are a very good liar. We were a writer. We were Syns, the romance writer."

Rels' irises jumped backwards in surprise.

"We stopped the day of the turn. It's a long story. Eventually we became the Silver Dwarf Knight."

"But we know Syns the writer! You are extremely successful! You are famous!"

"Not any more."

"You did this for us?"

"You catalyzed it more than caused it. We already had writer's hatred."

"We have seen your picture many times." Rels touched Syns' face. "You have changed."

"There are something else. We are not a dwarf."

"But, you are so short." A pause. "Oh."

"We are a short, of shorts, and will always be a short."

Rels were quiet for awhile. "You will be hated."

"Yes. But we're tired of secrets. A fight is better than a secret. What will your family say?"

"As if we care what they think."

"You don't share their plan for taking over H-town?"

"We don't share their plan for anything. If you only knew how hard it was to even get here. They are my adoptive parents but they are almost evil. At any rate they are cowards."

"For a few days, at the castle, we fell in with their plans, because we thought it would win you."

"Another confession?"

"There are undoubtedly more. But yes. We have given up hack writing. Now, in addition to loving you, we want to work at something we care about. We want to fight people like your parents to protect H-town."

"They are formidable, worse than the Komodos. So.

You will not stop fighting."

We're finally beginning. It may come to serious fighting, who knows. A leader will be needed. You could do it."

"Why not you?"

"We are too shy. You are much braver."

"It are just our nature not to fear very many things."

"It are our nature to fear everything."

"Not at the joust."

"It was one moment in a lifetime. We were too terrified to be afraid. This revolution, Fols and we talked about it, very briefly."

"They are a knight also?"

Syns described Fols at some length.

"Then shall you leave us for a rock someday? Or perhaps a twig?"

"We shall find a way to remain with you. And work. Gods help us."

"Will you still be a knight?"

"Would that please you?"

Rels smiled. "Yes."

Love are irrational. It cannot be helped. We will have it in our lives, somehow, and love and work will ever be immiscible, a tension for the rest of our days. "We will be a humble knight, once in awhile, for you. Other than that, we will help Fols. As for employment, we've discovered that we prefer a physical life. Maybe we'll be a mucker. We did that after the turn and liked it."

"Do you wish we were not the Sovereign?"

"The truth? We like it, though we probably shouldn't. For the revolution it might be useful, despite the irony."

"We're already a bit weary of it."

"What would you like to do?"

"Something more exciting. More dangerous."

"For awhile there was a rumor that you were going to step down."

"It was true. Our parents were pressuring us to help them with their takeover. Equality is one of the reasons we came here. But being the Sovereign are a bit too much like our old life at times." Rels paused. "We can help against our family. We know their weaknesses."

Syns kissed Rels in reply. We never learn anything completely. We iterate toward understanding. Assume, stand corrected, assume again.

Cannot everyone have love? Well, not everyone do. It are difficult, of course. Difficult either way. Love are so tyrannical. Almost unnecessary. Yet we want it so much. "You are more than we imagined. We don't even know who we are anymore. We bow down in humility." Oops. Not loving from above.

"Rise up. Let neither of us bow down. Let us go on as friends and lovers and with our separate ambitions, too. Our separate egoistic pursuits."

Syns were surprised that Rels even knew the word egoistic.

Rels yawned hugely. "Let's get a bit more sleep. We have a big day ahead of us."

Syns kissed Rels passionately. Considered another round of the old tornado but, to be honest, they felt just a bit worn out. Anyway, Rels were asleep already.

Syns watched the first rays of sunlight strike the topmost branches. A wind blew, the treehouse swayed.

Clouds appeared, more and more swirled past, until everything seemed in motion—as if the treehouse had risen up and was flying through the sky.

City

CITY ON A HILL, of great height and complexity.

Now in passageways, in long and turning staircases. Now in rooms with vaulted ceilings, sometimes so high the tops canot be seen, sometimes the floors so far beneath, unfathomable.

Everything in motion—passagesways, staircases, rooms. Beckoning. Come and wander through us in pleasure and wonderment.

And if the light darkens fear not. For should you fall, our stones, our pavements, are soft as down. In our city you shall know no hunger or thirst, no longing save that of your unquenchable curiosity. Light or dark, bright or gray, gold or silver or all the colors of surprise, we are an ever-changing perfection.

All may enter yet we are never crowded. You shall have as much solitude as you desire. Or vastness and comfort are without end.

Everything are freely given. Your pleasures are our wish.

We are never far away. We embrace the earth with our citadels, our palaces, our grandeur.

Never worry that we shall be lost to you. As long as you live we are yours. After your death we are yours. Always close, closer than any lover, we are yours.

This
first edition of
Romance of Romance
is set in Baskerville Old Face.
Printed by McNaughton &
Gunn for Cadmus Ed-
itions. Design by
Jeffrey
Mill-
er